AN INCONVENIENT
DEATH

RICHARD V. BARRY

Winterlight Books
Shelbyville, KY USA

AN INCONVENIENT DEATH
by Richard V. Barry

First Printing – October 2008
ISBN: 978-1-60047-254-1

Printed in the U.S.A.

THE LIFE WHICH IS UNEXAMINED IS NOT WORTH LIVING

SOCRATES

TO OFFICER MATT CAGGIANO

FOR: TECHNICAL ADVICE
PATIENT READING
LOYAL FRIENDSHIP

MANY THANKS

I

In 1994 I was forty-six and had been with the New York City Police Department for twenty-four years, having risen to the rank of detective lieutenant, when the Braxton case made national headlines and stirred gossip and speculation across the country.

David Braxton, oldest son of United States Senator Lawrence Braxton and heir to a huge pharmaceutical fortune, had, at forty-four, committed suicide while on a fishing trip in Idaho with his two best friends and Yale classmates. What made the case even more newsworthy was who those two Yale classmates were: Peter Campion, a rising television journalist and son of a famous movie actress of the fifties, Jessica Hunter; and Jack Mason III, from one of the oldest and richest New England families, a noted yachtsman and former captain of the United States Olympic Equestrian Team.

It's odd how people whom you've never met, you seem to know because you've read or heard so much about them. That's the way it was for me with these three guys. All three were used to the glare of publicity from the moment of birth to Braxton's death. When they graduated from Yale, Braxton and Campion had been co-valedictorians and Mason was right behind them. I remembered their achievement because at the time I was going to Queens College at night and barely making a B average. All three had also been elected to the Phi Beta Kappa honors society, as well as the mysterious and exclusive Skull and Bones society, while I was delighted to eventually become a Flesh and Blood graduate of Queens, with a C+ average.

Sunday newspaper supplements had written feature stories on the three of them, all best friends since their years at Groton together. I had never even heard of Groton, the fancy boarding school for rich kids, until I read about these guys. Actually I didn't read that much about them but I was given a running commentary on their lives by my first wife, Carolyn.

"Talk about being born with the silver spoon!" Carolyn commented after finishing an article about them, and I just nodded, not interested in hearing her go on about the glorious lives of the rich and famous. She really envied them and always wanted more than I could give her, which is one of the reasons we finally broke up. She's remarried to a guy who owns a Toyota dealership and she seems happier than when we were together. My second wife, Ginny, was content with what we had and we were really happy until her breast cancer struck and spread quickly into her lymph system and finally took her life a year ago.

After graduating from Yale, all three had immediately enlisted in the army during the Vietnam War and were saluted in newspapers across the country as outstanding examples of patriotism for young men of such high caliber and privilege to fight for their country. I guessed that meant that slobs like me who had been drafted to fight in Vietnam were undeserving of any special praise, yet I felt sure that I valued my ass just as much as these three men valued theirs.

It had again been front-page news when, more than a decade later, David Braxton married Nadira, the extraordinarily beautiful supermodel. They had three beautiful kids—at least they looked beautiful in the newspaper and magazine shots—a girl and twin boys. At the time of Braxton's death, I was forty-six, just two years older than the deceased. In investigating the life of David Braxton, I was struck by the irony that except for both of us being around the same age, male, Vietnam veterans, fathers and New Yorkers, our lives were so different that one of us could have come from Mars.

Peter Campion had also made headlines when he married a young Broadway actress, Margaret Shaw, who, in her mid-twenties had already won a Tony award as best supporting actress in a drama. My first wife had watched the awards show on television and, knowing that I didn't give a rat's ass about such things, insisted on telling me about it the next morning.

"She's married to that Peter Campion who they made such a fuss about when he graduated from Yale," she reported as she fed the baby and I finished my coffee. "She thanked him for all his support and the camera kept showing him sitting in the audience. He's really a handsome guy!" She said some more but I tuned her out as I rinsed my coffee cup in the sink, kissed our kids goodbye and headed out the door.

The lodge—the rich like to give rustic names to their palatial digs, thinking it makes them seem like just plain folk—the lodge where Braxton died was owned by his father but Senator Braxton seldom used it, while the three amigos spent two weeks there every spring—no wives or children, just a men's retreat for fishing and hunting and unwinding and, I guess, renewing old, strong ties. It was near Copper Canyon and the Copper River, renowned in the spring for its fly fishing after the snow from the mountains melted. The nearest town was about twenty miles away and the local sheriff and two deputies had their hands full with all the news people descending on the area, poking around and asking everyone questions, looking for some juicy news that would throw some light on why this guy who had everything would off himself. This is where I entered the case, about four days after Braxton's death.

Because all three men lived in New York City, Senator Braxton—who didn't represent our state but, what the hell, had clout anyway—requested that a New York City detective be assigned to the case. The Senator refused to believe that his son had committed suicide. I was picked since I had been the lead detective in solving a couple of high profile murders in the Big Apple that caught the public's attention. I visited my three kids who, by then, were living with my ex-wife and were with me only on alternate weekends, said goodbye and headed for Idaho. I figured it was an open and shut case and my confirming David Braxton's suicide would help the Senator accept the facts. I could never have imagined the bizarre twists this case would take as I wandered through the worlds of the rich and powerful, the privileged and the celebrated, nor could I have foreseen its profound effect on my own life.

II

After a two-hour drive from the airport to the small town nearest to the Braxton lodge, I met the local sheriff. His name was Tom Corrigan and he was just what you pictured when you thought of a small-town western sheriff: tall, at least three inches taller than my six feet, with a powerful upper body and the beginning of a paunch, a ruddy, pitted complexion and heavy creases around his eyes from squinting in the sun too much. Tom looked to be in his late forties and had a slow, measured way of speaking that left you hanging with anticipation for his next thought. He had a warm, open smile and a casual, relaxed manner that made me like him immediately. His two deputies were nice kids, just learning the job.

"I've never seen so many people," Tom said in his slow, baritone voice, "poken and proddin and askin questions and buzzen around like flies after honey."

"Well, this case is getting a lot of attention," I said, "because of the well-known people involved."

"I guess so," Tom said, squinting out the window of his cramped office into the sunshine. "Senator Braxton was here to claim the body. Boy, what a circus that was! The reporters and television crews have just about all left now."

"Was an autopsy performed?" I asked.

"Sure was," Tom said. "The coroner from Boise flew in."

"Anything unusual found?"

"Not a thing! No drugs. No diseases. A minor amount of alcohol but Campion and Mason said they had all been having a few drinks before dinner and we found glasses with the fingerprints of all three men on the living room coffee table and a bottle of Jack Daniels. The guy seemed to be in perfect health— clean as a whistle!"

Tom put his feet up on his cluttered desk, displaying worn boots.

"Makes you wonder, don't it? This guy had everything to live for!"

"So it seems," I said, "but if he did kill himself, there has to be a reason and we have to find it."

"Well," Tom said, shifting his gaze to me, "there's no doubt that he killed himself, so good luck finding the reason! I don't pretend to know anything about the rich and famous and how they operate and what makes them tick."

"Any servants at the lodge?"

"A local lady, Mrs. Jenkowski, who serves as a cook-housekeeper when anybody stays there, but it was her night off."

"What about the weapon?" I asked.

"A thirty-eight revolver, empty except for the bullet that killed him, which showed he meant business. He puts one shell in, brings the gun to his temple and off he goes."

"Was a forensic report made on the gun?"

"Sure was," Tom said, reaching toward the many papers piled on his desk and instantly taking an envelope from the top of one pile. "It just came in yesterday. Nothing unusual:"

He extracted the report from the envelope and handed it to me.

"In addition to Braxton's fingerprints," I said, quickly skimming the report, "there was a print identified as belonging to Campion."

"Yeah," Tom said matter-of-factly. "The gun was kept at the lodge in a desk drawer, and Campion said he had moved it when he was looking for some writing paper."

"Did he say he took it out of the drawer or did he just move it inside the drawer?" I asked, having seen something in the report that caught my attention.

"I don't remember that detail from when I questioned him, but I've got all my notes on the case here," Tom said, bending his body forward to open the top drawer of his battered desk and producing a set of neatly typed papers. "Here it is," he said and he began to read from his notes.

"Question: Did you know about the gun that Mr. Braxton used to kill himself? Campion: Yes, it was always kept in a drawer in David's desk in the den. Question: When was the last time you saw it? Campion: About two or three days before David shot himself. Question: How did you come to see it? Campion: I was looking for some writing paper and opened the drawer and saw the gun. I had seen it many times before. Question: Where specifically was the gun located? Campion: In the top middle drawer. Question: Did you touch it? Campion: Yes, I believe I did. I'm quite sure I moved it out of the way to get the writing paper that was underneath it. Question: Are you used to handling guns? Campion: Guns, no, not since my army days over twenty years ago. Hunting rifles, yes."

"He moved it out of the way," I repeated what Tom had just read to me and Tom nodded. "The report said that Campion's thumbprint was found on the lower part of the handle of the gun," I said, thinking aloud, "but if you were rummaging in a drawer looking for some writing paper, how would anyone usually grab a gun?"

Tom thought for a moment before answering and a tight little smile formed on his lips.

"You'd probably grab it by the barrel because your inclination, unless you really know guns, would be to stay away from the trigger."

"And," I added to Tom's thought, "if you did move it by the handle—say you were shoving it to one side—you would do this with your whole hand, so why was only Campion's thumbprint on the handle?"

"Because David Braxton's prints were on top of the rest of Campion's prints?" Tom speculated.

"But his thumbprint was on the flat side of the handle. That's not how you'd grasp a gun to slide it to one side."

"You're right," Tom said, shaking his head, "but maybe he picked it up momentarily to get it out of the way."

"Possibly," I said, "but if you're not used to handling guns, as Campion admitted, wouldn't the natural thing be to slide it out of the way?"

"I guess so," Tom conceded with a slight chuckle. "You big city detectives leave no stone unturned, do you?"

"Well, this is an interesting detail I'll file away," I said, smiling back at Tom. "Can I get a copy of all your notes?"

Tom's smile broadened as he thrust the typed pages he'd been holding toward me.

"Here they are!" he said. "I had my wife type them up last night."

"Thank you," I said, taking the papers from his large, outstretched hand, "and thank your wife. When can I visit the lodge?"

Tom took his feet off his desk and stood up, stretching his tall frame.

"Why don't you look those over and then first thing tomorrow morning I'll drive you out there."

"Great!" I said, rising to leave.

"Oh, I almost forgot," Tom said hastily. "My wife wants you to come for supper tonight. She says you won't get a decent meal otherwise. About six o'clock."

"I gladly accept," I said, never having thought about food since arriving at this tiny town a few hours ago and checking in at the one shabby motel.

"Come by here at five-forty-five when I finish for the day," Tom said.

We shook hands and I left his office, walking the short distance to my motel room where I immediately sat on the bed and began reading Tom's notes. At times like this I craved a cigarette, but I had given them up the week before. And the week before that, and the week before that! I knew there was half a pack in the back of my suitcase, just for emergencies like this, and I quickly found them and was happily puffing away again, resolving to give them up for good as soon as I finished this pack.

III

Since both Peter Campion and Jack Mason had flown back to New York with Senator Braxton and his son's body, I wasn't able to question anyone directly connected with the death, so I read Tom's notes and was duly impressed with his thoroughness. The three men came every year about this time for a few weeks' stay, devoted to hunting and fishing. The suicide took place on the last full day of their visit at about 6 P.M. when Braxton, seated in the living room, fired one shot from the thirty-eight revolver into the side of his head, killing him instantly. Both Campion and Mason were in their rooms on the second floor when they heard a shot and came rushing down to find Braxton slumped across the sofa in front of the fireplace, still clutching the gun.

The sheriff's office was notified at approximately 7 P.M. with Deputy Wexler taking the call and the sheriff and both deputies arrived on the scene at 7:30 P.M. They could find no suicide note. Tom noted that both Campion and Mason seemed very distressed and shocked and that Mason broke down whenever he tried to talk. After getting the basic facts, mostly from Campion, the sheriff notified the coroner, took pictures of the scene and arranged to question Mason and Campion further the next day. Both men agreed to meet Tom at his office the following afternoon.

Still visibly upset but much more composed, they said they had no idea why Braxton had committed suicide. He had never given any indication of being depressed or upset during the previous days they had spent together at the lodge, or even on the day of his death. They had gathered in the living room for drinks after a day of fly fishing in a nearby stream and then Campion and Mason had gone to their rooms—Mason to take a brief nap, which was his customary habit, and Campion to write a letter. They could offer no possible explanation for this horrible turn of events, and Mason kept repeating, "This never should have happened."

I lay back on the bed, replaying the scene in my mind. Tom's notes were good but I could see some gaps—some questions that hadn't been asked and needed answering. Details were bothering me. Why would anyone deciding to commit suicide do it in the most public area of the house: the living room? And why would you choose 6 P.M. after what the two other men described as a good fishing day and a happy cocktail hour? And why would a guy who had everything to live for—a beautiful wife and three kids and wealth and position—suddenly take his life and give no explanation—leave no note to his family? It just didn't add up. I got up, showered and headed back to Tom's office for dinner at his house.

IV

Tom's house, about three miles outside of town, was a typical ranch style, nestled in a grove of trees, set back far from the road. Inside, it was warm and cozy and his wife's touch was evident everywhere.

This is George Russo," Tom said quietly as I extended my hand to Lily.

Lily Corrigan was a fine looking woman, tall like her husband and on the buxom side but shapely. I always liked a woman with some meat on her bones and my first wife, Carolyn, had a great shape, like Lily's, until she decided she wanted to look like those models in the fashion magazines and began starving herself after our kids were born.

She'd make a regular dinner for me and the kids and then I'd watch her eating a plate of lettuce, celery and carrot sticks. It was like living with a rabbit! At parties, on vacations, celebrating special events, she never let up on her fanatical diet and had memorized the calories of every food, in all combinations, known to man. She even became a food voyeur, delighting in watching me and the kids consume meals that I knew she had formerly loved. Our kids started to look like little sausages and my waistline expanded while hers shrunk. Now, when I go to pick up the kids and she wants to tell me something, she looks like a walking, talking stick.

Ginny, my second wife, was round where a woman should be round and she loved to cook and always joked about losing a few pounds after her next birthday, but she knew I loved her just as she was: soft and warm, with enticing curves, mounds and crevices, a body to get lost in and then snuggle against. Lily had clear blue eyes that actually seemed to twinkle, fair skin and hair and a generous mouth that was now shaped in a huge smile. After greeting us at the door, escorting us to the living room and giving us both a beer, Lily excused herself to finish preparing the dinner, and Tom and I settled into two leather chairs by the lit fireplace. Tom offered me a cigarette. Now there are few things that go better with a cigarette than coffee or a drink. I hesitated for only a moment before accepting the offered cigarette.

"I've been trying to give them up," I admitted with a guilty grin.

"Well, remember what Mark Twain said about giving up smoking," Tom said, lighting his own cigarette. "It's the easiest thing in the world. He did it at least a thousand times."

We both laughed and made small talk for a short time before I changed the subject.

"Tom, look at us sitting here, enjoying a drink at the start of the evening. Does it make any sense to you that a guy with everything to live for would kill himself—for whatever reason—in his living room at this particular time of day?"

Tom responded with "No, not a damn bit, but it's out of my hands now and while I can't make any sense of it, he did kill himself and I'm not gonna lose any sleep over it."

"It just doesn't add up," I said, after taking a swig of my beer. "unless the guy was an acute manic-depressive and had uncontrollable mood swings and decided on the spur of the moment to kill himself."

Tom nodded but said nothing.

"I'll check into his medical history when I get back to New York," I said, more to myself than to Tom.

We drank our beers in a comfortable silence, staring at the logs burning in the fireplace, until Lily announced that dinner was ready and we moved into the large kitchen where an attractively decorated round oak table was set for four. In answer to my unasked question, a tall young man appeared and was introduced as Tom and Lily's nineteen-year-old son, Keith.

Dinner was delicious and reminded me of the meals Ginny, my second wife, used to make. Lily served fried chicken and dumplings and mashed potatoes and gravy and sweet corn and salad and even home-made biscuits.

"George, there's a rule in this house," Lily said with one of her big smiles. "If you like my cooking, you have to have seconds."

"A very sensible rule!" I replied.

I needed no coaxing and refilled my plate with more of everything as Lily made small gestures of encouragement.

Keith, even taller than his father but with a stockier frame and his mother's smile, asked a lot of questions about big-city detective work, and while both Tom and Lily told Keith not to ask so many questions and to let me eat in peace, I could sense that all three were interested in my stories and descriptions. Home-made apple pie with ice cream was served along with coffee as we chatted easily and the evening passed quickly. I said goodnight around 9:30 and Tom drove me back to the motel.

"The thing that puzzles me the most," Tom said suddenly after we had been driving in silence for some time, "is the absence of a suicide note."

"It would suggest that his suicide was strictly a spur-of-the-moment decision," I said, "with no forethought. But that happens rarely and usually with people who have long histories of mental problems."

"The funny thing is," said Tom, as if thinking to himself, "nobody finished his drink."

"What's that?" I asked, my ears perking up.

"All the glasses on the coffee table in the living room had some Jack Daniels left in them. We dusted for fingerprints and found the full prints of each man on the three glasses."

"On all three glasses?" I asked quickly

"No," Tom said, shaking his head. "Just a full set of different prints on each of the three glasses, showing that all three men had been drinking and no one had finished his last drink. Just left them there on the coffee table."

"And what do you make of that?" I asked.

"I don't know what the hell to make if it," Tom said, his face clouded with confusion. "George, I haven't dealt with a murder or a suicide case in more than twenty years—not since Bobby Johnson came back from Vietnam and everyone saw that his whole personality had changed and he stayed in his room at his parents' house for weeks on end and then hung himself in the barn in the dead of night. He left a note to his parents that they never shared with us but we knew it was a clear-cut case of suicide and we didn't push it. But this!"

His voice trailed off.

"I know," I said. "This has puzzling loose ends. Too many! Did you check the content of the three glasses?"

Tom smiled. "George, we're not complete rubes," he said. "Of course we did! Straight Jack Daniels in Braxton and Campion's glasses and a little water added to Mason's drink."

We fell into another silence as both of us tried to fit the pieces of the puzzle together and I had the feeling that some pieces were still missing.

V

The next morning, I had breakfast at the only diner along the main street, which made me doubly grateful for Lily's home cooking the night before. Then I walked to Tom's office one block north, enjoying my first cigarette of the day and promising myself that the pack I had just bought at the diner would be my last. Tom was outside his office, waiting for me, and we drove out to the Braxton lodge, about a half-hour away.

As I had pretty much expected, the lodge was on a vast tract of land, "about seven hundred acres," Tom told me, "mostly left wild except for a clearing around the main building." We stopped in front of a tall metal gate and Tom got out and unlocked it. We drove between thick woods on each side of the winding dirt road for a long stretch. We crossed a meadow where the road almost disappeared and, with Tom's pickup in low gear, drove up a steep, wooded incline until we came upon the multi-arch-roofed lodge, sitting in proud isolation midway up some mountainous foothills. As we approached it, the lodge looked to be of modest size, but I quickly saw on closer inspection that the first appearance was deceptive because there were two long wings that extended away from the rear of the building.

We entered a soaring foyer with a massive oak staircase leading to the second story and walked past a large dining room where, visible behind that, there was a sparkling state-of-the-art kitchen. Tom led me immediately into the living room running along the back of the main wing, with nothing but windows forming the rear wall, giving us an eye-popping view of majestic mountains above us in the distance.

I thought of all the suburban houses that now had a designated "great room," which was a joke when compared to what I was standing in. This room I judged to be at least fifty feet long and twenty feet wide, with a double-height ceiling and heavy, exposed beams reaching a peak of probably thirty feet.

The room was divided by several groupings of furniture. While the exposed timbers and western style furnishings and paintings suggested rusticity, the vast expanse of the house, with two rambling one-story wings extending off the long two-story main house, reflected the wealth it represented. In front of a massive river-rock fireplace, flanked by two wing-back leather chairs, was a long over-stuffed sofa and large, oak plank coffee table with the three half-empty glasses, the bottle of Jack Daniels, two small dishes, one with peanuts and one with pretzels, and nothing else.

I quickly surveyed the scene and saw the dried blood stains on the sofa where Braxton had died. The stains were on both the back of the sofa where he had shot himself and on the seat cushion where his body had slumped over. From the position of the three glasses I noted that Campion and Mason must have been sitting in the wing-back chairs, facing Braxton who was sitting alone on the sofa when they were having their drinks. I walked over to the fireplace.

"Tom, to your knowledge, has anyone touched anything since Braxton's death?"

"No. The housekeeper asked me if she should come in and clean up but I said not until you had a chance to inspect everything."

I gazed down at the neatly arranged logs and the kindling in the fireplace.

"So on the evening of Braxton's death," I said, thinking out loud, "the three buddies gather at the cocktail hour for a few relaxing drinks but they don't bother to light the fire in the fireplace that's already been prepared for them. Curious!"

Tom made no reply.

"Where's the den where the gun was usually kept?" I asked.

Tom led me through a door at the far end of the room, into another, smaller room with oak paneling. He pointed to a massive, old roll-top desk in a corner. I approached the desk and opened the top middle drawer.

"Didn't Campion tell you that the gun was kept in this drawer, Tom?"

"That's right: the top middle drawer."

I examined the few contents of the drawer.

"And he said that he had shifted the gun's position because he was getting at some writing paper that was under it, right?" I said.

"Right," Tom replied, standing beside me and peering down at the open drawer.

"But there's no writing paper here!" I said.

"Perhaps he took it all," Tom offered.

"Possibly," I said and closed the drawer. "Do we know where the three men's bedrooms were, Tom?"

"Yes, we checked them out," Tom said, with just a hint of pride in his voice.

"Let's have a look," I said.

I followed Tom out to the high-ceiling foyer and up the massive oak staircase with intricately curved iron balustrades. On reaching the second floor landing there was a long corridor with dormered windows running along the front of the house and evenly spaced doors on the opposite side.

"All three of them had their rooms along this corridor," Tom explained. "The other two wings were kept closed unless Senator Braxton came with a big party."

Tom identified the door nearest to the stairs as Braxton's room. In this room, even more than in the downstairs public rooms, the unmistakable look of quiet luxury was everywhere, reminding me in a fleeting flashback of all the pictures of palatial interiors in Architectural Digest that my first wife used to shove under my nose from time to time to show me how people more ambitious than I was, could live.

The ornately carved king-size bed, the tan, suede bedcover that matched a tan suede wall covering, a large fireplace with a comfortable leather club chair beside it, the three large oil paintings of vast western landscapes, the heavy drapes at the windows, the enormous adjacent marble bathroom with a huge soaking tub, double sink and a separate steam shower—everything said that money was no object and no price was spared. When I compared all this to the twelve-by-eleven-foot bedroom my ex-wife and I had shared, with the one cramped bathroom down the hall where the wife, kids and I had to line up in the morning to take our turns, I couldn't blame her for dreaming about something better.

The bed was flanked by two nightstands and on one of them I saw a book. I walked over and examined it: a beautiful leather-bound copy of *Walden* by Henry David Thoreau. I flipped through the pages quickly and in doing so, something caught my eye, so I flipped through them again until I found it. A passage had been neatly underlined in red ink. I read it.

"I did not want to come to the end of my life and find that I had not lived."

Now I'm not much of a reader, except for John Grisham and Robert Ludlum, but I do like to watch PBS sometimes when there aren't any good sports programs on, and I remembered seeing a special on Thoreau and how he moved to a hut next to Walden Pond because he wanted to really get back to basics. How ironic, I thought, looking at the underlined passage, that this book was being read and, from the underlining, taken to heart, in such a rich setting.

If Braxton had underlined this passage, what could it tell me? Maybe that despite his wealth and position, he longed for a simple life—something he knew he could never achieve? For all his good fortune, was he basically unhappy and inwardly brooding, which no one seemed to have detected? Of course, I reminded myself, this was all pure speculation, but as a good detective I had to be open to many speculations in order to find the right key to this puzzle. I copied the underlined passage in my pocket-size notebook and returned the *Walden* book to the nightstand.

"They certainly lived well while they were roughing it, didn't they?" I said, surveying the large, comfortable bedroom once more.

Tom just smiled and led me to the bedroom next to Braxton's, which Mason occupied. While not quite as large as the master's, it, too, was luxuriously appointed—a phrase I picked up from a newspaper's reporting on a Park Avenue homicide I had been investigating when I first became a detective. In that case, the wife's lover turned out to be the handsome young Irish doorman of their fancy apartment building who killed the millionaire husband at the wife's urging. They were both convicted. It was my first big case.

Mason's bedroom had a private bath, as did Campion's, which was the third bedroom in the row. I noticed a curious architectural detail about all three bedrooms we had visited: the one large window in each room faced out on the double-height living room which ran the length of the main wing, and most of the natural light came from large skylights centered over the bed in each room and over the soaking tube in each bathroom. When I opened the window in Campion's room, I was looking directly down on the living room, with the sofa where Braxton had died in plain sight.

"They could easily have heard the single shot from their bedrooms," I said, thinking aloud again, "but if they had been any place near their windows, they could have looked down and seen Braxton in the act of killing himself. A suicide hardly wants an audience unless he isn't really serious about it In that case, he goes to a bridge and threatens to jump off and then gets talked out of it."

I turned back to face Tom who only nodded. I was crossing Campion's bedroom, heading toward the door when I spotted something. On a small desk lay a flat leather case with the initials PMC in gold letters on the cover. I opened the case and found heavy stationery on one side, with Peter Morley Campion embossed at the top of each page, and on the other side of the case, matching envelopes with a Fifth Avenue address printed on the back.

"This is Campion's personal stationery," I announced to Tom "He must have forgotten it when he left."

"He was really upset from what I saw of him," Tom said.

"Or," I replied quickly, "maybe he always kept it here because this was his semi-permanent room each year when the three men came for their annual outing."

"That could be," Tom agreed.

"But why was he searching for writing paper in the desk in the den where the gun was kept? Isn't that what he claimed?"

Tom thought for a moment before responding.

"That's right," he said, then paused before adding, "but maybe he was looking for some plain paper to write something other than a letter."

"Yes," I said, "but I remember from your notes that I read last night—and they were very good, by the way—that Campion's answer to your question about how he had come to see and touch the gun was because he was looking for some 'writing paper.' He did specify 'writing paper,' didn't he, Tom? Not just 'paper' or 'scratch paper' or 'plain paper' but 'writing paper.'"

"Well now, George," Tom said with a half-teasing smile, "there are all kinds of writing besides letter writing, you know. Maybe he wanted to scribble some notes—remember, he's a television reporter—or maybe he wanted to outline an idea for some future story. Or maybe he wanted to scribble a list of things he had to do when he returned to New York the next day. Remember, they were at the end of their vacation and were scheduled to fly home the next morning. I don't think you can make too much of the writing case here,"

"Except that today there wasn't one piece of paper of any kind in that drawer where the gun was kept," I shot back. "And he said he had to move the gun because he saw the paper under it."

"Maybe there were only a few pieces of paper and he took them all," Tom said.

"Possibly," I said, with little conviction. All the possibilities were leading me nowhere and I was visibly frustrated. I looked at my watch and saw that I had just five hours before my flight to New York. Considering the two-hour car ride back to the airport and giving myself at least forty-five minutes at the airport, that left me only about two hours.

"Lily wants you to come for lunch," Tom said. "She and Keith really took to you. And besides," he added with a chuckle, "we want to spare you the cholesterol buildup you'd get from any lunch at Pop's Diner. Keith announced this morning that he thinks you're cool and he'd like to be a big city detective and not a rube like his dad, stuck out here in the unexciting boonies."

"I'd take the unexciting boonies anytime," I said, "if I didn't have kids to support."

We drove back to Tom's home as I bragged about my three great kids: Emily, nineteen, George Jr., sixteen, and Beth, twelve.

"Beth is the musical one: she sings and plays piano and clarinet and wants to either go on the stage or be a music teacher. Georgie is a typical teenager: rebellious and sullen one minute, loving and high spirited the next. He's already six-foot-three and his hormones are going crazy. Emily's special talent is mothering me. She worries about me and is always telling me what to take for a cold or asking me if I'm eating the right foods. And she hates that I smoke and is always lecturing me about it."

"I quit eight years ago, on my fortieth birthday," Tom said, "and it was one of the hardest things I ever did. But Lily was very supportive, and I lasted for almost two years Then she had an operation for some female problems and complications developed, and she was laid up for a long time and I fell back into the habit."

"You're right," I agreed, "It sure as hell isn't easy. I've gone for a couple of weeks but then some occasion arises—a party or a bowling night with the boys or some tense situation connected with work or simply a craving for the ritual of smoking—and I'm back to square one."

"Keep trying," Tom urged as we pulled into the driveway of his house, and Lily was again at the door to greet us.

"George, Senator Lawrence's office in Washington has been trying to contact you. He wants you to call him as soon as possible."

Tom directed me to a small room at the back of the house that he used as a den, and I dialed the number in Washington D.C. A pleasant female voice said "Senator Braxton's office." I gave my name and said I was returning the Senator's call and was put through to another pleasant female voice but this one deeper and with an air of command.

"Mr. Russo, the Senator was just called to the floor to vote on a bill. Can he call you back within the hour?"

"Yes," I said, "but it can't be any longer than that because I'm leaving to catch a plane."

"Well, it shouldn't be very long," the authoritative voice said. "I'll have him call you as soon as he returns. He'll call you on his private line. Is there any privacy where you are?"

"Yes," I said.

"Good! Please wait as long as you can. If he misses you, call him when you get to the airport."

She gave me the Senator's private number at his office and also his number at his house in Washington.

"He's very, very anxious to speak to you," she said before hanging up.

I guessed the wheels of power were moving slowly because the Senator didn't call in the next fifty minutes and I had to say goodbye to Lily and Tom and Keith, return to my motel, pay my bill, pick up my bag and drive the two hours to the airport. At the airport I tried his private office number and when there was no answer, I called his house number but a lady with a thick southern accent said that he wasn't at home.

VI

On the plane back to New York I kept playing the scene of the suicide over and over. Three brilliant, successful and celebrated young men,—I flattered myself that mid-forties was still young—boyhood friends, return to Idaho for their annual manly retreat and on the last night of their stay are having a few drinks in the living room. They don't light the fire in the fireplace that's already prepared; they don't finish their drinks; two depart for their rooms with direct visual access to the living room and the third remains on the sofa and puts a bullet through his head.

Questions were spinning in my head. When did Braxton get the gun? Where was the gun while the three of them were having drinks? Did Braxton have any history of mental instability? Did Braxton have any secret vices? Any marital problems? Any hidden friction between the three? Is there some gay angle here? Not likely, I quickly told myself, from all the celebrated romances all three men had racked up before they all married in their thirties. Still, a small possibility. I had been on a case where the husband and the stepson had become lovers and murdered the wife for her money.

I re-read Tom's notes and they generated more questions. How long between the two men leaving the living room and their hearing the shot? How long between hearing the shot and notifying the sheriff? Who else did they notify? I made a note to ask Campion to describe in detail how he moved the gun in the drawer, and to follow up with Mason on what he meant when he kept saying "This shouldn't have happened," when the sheriff arrived. There were too many unanswered questions, too many inconsistencies. My gut was churning by the time my plane touched down in New York, and I bought another pack of cigarettes before leaving the airport, vowing that this would be my last.

VII

That evening, after a quick supper of a frozen pizza and a can of corn—I never cooked during the years of my two marriages, except to make salads and barbecue in the summer, and I had no desire to learn now—I dialed the Senator's home number.

"The Braxton residence," announced the female voice on the other end, clearly a servant.

"This is George Russo calling for Senator Braxton," I said, omitting the detective lieutenant in identifying myself. "He's expecting my call."

"Just a minute, please."

But it was several minutes before I heard the familiar baritone voice of Senator Braxton, well known to most Americans as the senior member and spokesman of the minority party. He began by thanking me for getting back to him so promptly and as he spoke these few lines I noted a strained tiredness in his voice. He sounded old and defeated.

"Have you discovered anything, Mr. Russo? " the Senator asked in a half-pleading tone.

"Well, sir, there are a lot of unanswered questions and a number of confusing details about your son's suicide."

The Senator interrupted me and his voice grew stronger.

"My son did not commit suicide!" he said emphatically. "There's absolutely no reason why my son would take his own life!"

"I understand, sir," I said, but wanted to move on to more specific topics. "What I'm trying to do now is to rule out all the possibilities that might support a suicide theory. To your knowledge, did your son have any health problems?"

"David? Hell, no! He was in perfect health.

"What about financial worries? Maybe some significant loss in investments?

"No!" was the Senator's quick reply. "My three oldest children are in the fortunate position of having very large trust funds left to them by my father, and David, as the first grandson, has the largest of all. As a matter of fact, I know that David had recently made a killing in the market and was actually better situated than probably anyone else in our family."

I loved the way that Senator Braxton modestly described his son's being "better situated." The newspapers were estimating his worth at nearly a billion dollars. I switched to another subject.

"Any marital problems that you know of, Senator?" I asked, and his response came without hesitation

"None! David and Nadira were very, very happy! She gave up her career when they married and she has devoted herself to her family. She's an outstanding mother!" Then he added, "I love Nadira."

"Senator, can you think of anything in your son's personality that might suggest a dark side—an inclination to depression or moroseness?"

"Lieutenant. Russo," the Senator said, a tone of resentment overlaying his words, "my son was just about the sunniest, most balanced man you could ever meet. He was that way from the time he was just a baby and his positive disposition only increased as an adult."

There was a slight pause and then the Senator continued. "I remember when he was at Yale and he was majoring in philosophy and we'd talk on the phone every week and he used to say, 'Dad, we should all live our lives as if each day was out last.'"

I jotted down that line in my notebook.

The Senator's voice seemed to grow weaker as he quoted his son and I thought he might be going to cry, but he seemed to regain his composure and he said in a stronger voice, "And that's the way he always lived his life. Each day was a new adventure, a new challenge to live to the fullest and experience as much as possible, taking delight in big and small events, relishing every minute. He had this huge appetite for relishing every moment and he infected others with his enthusiasm for living."

He paused again and now his voice had a definite tremor and ascended to a higher pitch. "No one valued life more than my son and that's why it's incredible! No one who knew him believes that he would take his life. No one! It's a violation of everything he believed in, everything he practiced."

"Senator, what are your thoughts on Peter Campion and Jack Mason?"

"Peter and Jack and my son were as close as brothers from the time they were at Groton together. When they all went to Yale, David convinced Peter to be a philosophy major, like him. Jack stayed in pre-law but he took a lot of philosophy courses too. They supported each other in everything. I think David felt closer to them than to his own siblings. They were like a secret society all to themselves. Even their wives would say that. From the time they were kids together at Groton they called themselves the 'seeing ones,' whatever that means, and whenever David would be talking to either Jack or Peter on the phone, he'd always end the conversation with 'carpe diem.'"

I scribbled the words in my notebook.

"Seize the day!" I said automatically, having had Latin as part of my Catholic education.

"Yes," said the Senator, "and if you look at the lives of these boys, you can see that that's what they all did: Seize the day!"

Now I hit him with the big question.

"Senator, how do you account for both Campion and Mason's saying it was suicide?"

A long pause and when he spoke again, the desperation was clearly apparent in the Senator's voice.

"I can't…I don't know why they would say that, knowing him as they did and being as positively charged about life as he was, and…there has to be some other explanation…something that's been overlooked…there just has to be!"

"Here's a possible scenario," I said, introducing an idea I had been playing with since my flight back to New York. "Suppose the three men were sitting around, having a few drinks and being silly as buddies can be at any age, and they started playing around with the gun and they didn't know there was one bullet in the chamber and your son, as a joke, put it to his head and accidentally discharged it?"

"Yes, yes, that's possible," the Senator said, his voice rising, "and in their shock and surprise they were too embarrassed to admit it."

"Or," I said, continuing with another possibility, "suppose they had a few too many drinks and really got a little crazy and, in a macho challenge, were playing Russian roulette? That would account for the one bullet in the chamber."

"Definitely not!" the Senator shouted through the phone. "They would never be that reckless, that stupid! That would be a contradiction to everything they stood for… lived for… believed in."

"That didn't make much sense to me either," I admitted.

"Besides," the Senator said, "David didn't like guns and was always nervous around them ever since he was a boy and I was cleaning a gun and shot myself accidentally in the foot."

"But he was a hunter," I said.

"No he wasn't!" the Senator said. "Peter and Jack were hunters, but David was a fisherman and when the other two occasionally went hunting, David just fished. David told me that in the last couple of years both Peter and Jack had given up hunting."

"Weren't they all in the military and saw duty in Vietnam? I asked, recalling a bit of their celebrated biographies.

"Yes, but they were officers," was the Senator's almost scornful reply.

My mind flashed back to the living room at the Senator's lodge and the absence of any stuffed trophy animals.

"I'll get back to you, Senator, after I've talked to Campion and Mason."

"Please, Lieutenant Russo," the Senator said, his voice breaking again, "Please find the real cause of my son's death. Please."

"I'll do my best, Senator," I said.

"Call me anytime at this number," he said, "or use my private number at my office."

"I have that," I confirmed.

We said goodbye and I sat still long afterwards, planning my interviews with Campion and Mason, smoking my last three cigarettes in the pack and resolving once again that tomorrow would be the first day of my smoke-free life.

VIII

The private five-story townhouse in the east sixties between Madison and Lexington Avenues was a typical New York residence of the very rich. Both the façade and the interior had been modernized, losing all traces of its original design and character. This was the home of Jack Mason, his wife, Deirdre, and their two children, Garret and Penny.

I had called to arrange a meeting with Mason, which had been set for the afternoon after my phone conversation with Senator Braxton but then postponed by Mason twice. Now, two days later, I was seated across from Mason in a high-ceiling room on the "parlor" floor, one level up from the street level, and Mason, a striking looking patrician in features, carriage and dress, was clearly nervous. As I quickly surveyed the spacious, sleekly furnished room, I noticed the many family pictures taken on boats—most could only be called yachts, I thought—and on horseback that crowded the top of the grand piano, along with a picture of Mason's Olympic equestrian teammates.

"I just have some routine questions, Mr. Mason," I said in a casual way, trying to put him at ease.

Mason nodded but said nothing.

"Could you just tell me in your own words what happened the evening of Mr. Braxton's death?"

Mason, his legs crossed and arms folded across his chest, looked off into the distance and spoke in a low, halting cadence, as if he were trying to visualize that scene but also trying to sound casual.

"It was the last day of our vacation. We were flying back home the next day and it had been a great time for us—the fishing had been especially good. Mrs. Jenkowski had the evening off but she had made us a dinner in advance and we were in the living room having a drink. When we finished our drinks, I wanted to take a quick nap before dinner—I'm a habitual nap taker—and Peter wanted to write a letter, so we both went to up to our rooms, and David said he'd sit for a bit and then heat up the dinner. I dozed off and then I heard a loud bang and it woke me and I couldn't get my bearings for a moment but I heard Peter shout something like 'Oh, God, no!' and I got up and raced downstairs and Peter was standing over David's slumped body and there was blood everywhere."

Mason's voice faltered at this point and his eyes grew misty.

"Peter checked David's pulse and said he was dead."

Mason now looked directly at me for the first time.

"How long after you left the living room would you say it was before you heard the shot?" I asked.

Mason looked thoughtful.

"Oh, I guess it was about twenty minutes or thereabouts," he replied. "Why?"

"Just getting the right time frame for everything," I said, taking my notebook from my inside jacket pocket and slowly flipping the pages.

Mason uncrossed his legs and then crossed them again, with his hands cupped over his knee.

"How many drinks did you say you had?" I asked.

"I had two—I dilute mine with a little water—Peter had two, I think, and David had only one.

"How long would you say it was that the three of you were together having your drinks?"

"Probably no more than a half-hour," Mason said, turning his gaze away from me.

"And what time was it when you first gathered together for your drinks?"

Mason shifted his body in the modern, armless chair he was sitting in and cleared his throat.

"It was about five o'clock," he said quickly. "We came back to the lodge a little after four and we all wanted to take a shower and change our clothes and we agreed to meet at five."

I jotted a few numbers in my notebook before asking my next question.

"So if you came together at 5PM, and you spent about a half-hour together and then you were separated for about twenty minutes before hearing the shot, that puts the time of death a little before six, right?"

"Yes, that's about right," Mason agreed.

I flipped the notebook pages back to a previous section as Mason watched me intently.

"Now the sheriff said that he received a call at his office from Peter Campion at approximately 7 P.M., telling him of Mr. Braxton's death."

Mason shifted his weight again and looked expectantly at me but said nothing.

"That's at least an hour between the time you found the body and the time you called the sheriff. Why did you wait so long?"

Mason didn't answer right away and when he did, he had assumed a different air—one almost of condescension, I thought.

"Well, first of all, I can't say with any certitude exactly when we discovered David's body, so it may have been less than the hour you're claiming. Then, there was the total shock we both felt and it took us some time to even think straight."

I nodded my head as though in supportive agreement. His next lines were delivered in a definite tone of condescension, no doubt about it.

"David Braxton wasn't just anyone, Lieutenant Russo, and this horrible event was, I'm sure you'll agree, extraordinary. When we finally did recover our wits, we called Senator Braxton with the devastating news."

"Who called Senator Braxton?" I interrupted.

"Why, Peter," Mason said.

"Did you call anyone else?" I asked, staring down at my notes as if I already knew the answer, which I didn't.

"Yes, we called our wives so that they wouldn't first hear the horrible news on some television news program."

"Did you call David's wife?"

"No, Senator Braxton said he wanted to do that."

"Anyone else?"

Mason hesitated before answering, as if weighing his options.

"Yes, we called Professor Jenkins. He was our favorite philosophy professor at Yale and we were all quite close to him."

"So close that at such a tragic moment like this, you'd think of calling a favorite philosophy professor?" I asked, disbelief clearly evident in my tone.

"Look," Mason said, his voice rising in indignation and his words coming rapidly, "It may seem strange to you, even preposterous, but we were reeling from what had just happened to our best friend and, yes, in our dazed and confused state of mind we just needed to talk to Professor Jenkins, the one person we could trust."

"The one person you could trust?" I repeated.

Mason hesitated, then spoke in a milder tone.

"What I mean is, Professor Jenkins has such real wisdom and he had influenced all three of us profoundly and the thought just came into Peter's head and he mentioned it to me and I thought it was a good idea—we were clutching at straws here, you must understand—and we called him and he was home and Peter spoke to him first and then I did."

"For how long?" I asked

"Oh, just a short time. I don't know precisely," Mason said irritably, glancing at his watch.

"Did you call anyone else before calling the sheriff?" I asked, jotting in my notebook to check the phone log for the lodge that evening.

"Peter called his family's lawyer," Mason said flatly.

"Why would he do that?"

"I really don't know. Perhaps Professor Jenkins had suggested it. I don't honestly remember."

"What did the lawyer say?"

Mason gave me a smirk. "I'm afraid you'll have to ask that question of Peter," he said, rising from his chair.

"I will," I said assertively, "but just one more question for you, Mr. Mason."

Mason leaned his head forward like some lord listening to a peasant.

"You and Mr. Braxton and Mr. Campion used to call yourselves 'the seeing ones.' What did you mean by that?"

For the first time Mason looked very uncomfortable and tried to cover his dismay with a forced smile while his eyes circled the room and he folded his arms across his chest.

"That was just a childish game we played," he said, continuing his forced smile.

"And what did it mean?" I asked, refusing to give ground.

"Oh, I hardly remember. Something about the all-seeing eye of Buddha, as I vaguely recall. We were always reading about strange beliefs and incorporating them into our adolescent games and fantasies."

I flipped the pages in my notebook. "You told me that after the three of you had finished your drinks, you and Mr. Campion went to your rooms, right?"

"That's correct," Mason said, impatience creeping into his voice.

"But when the sheriff and I visited the lodge, we found that all three glasses that bore the fingerprints of you three gentlemen still had whiskey in them. How do you explain that?"

Mason suddenly stood up and a look of confusion came into his eyes.

"Explain what?" he said.

"You told me that all three of you finished your drinks but, in fact, none of you had."

Mason looked around the room as though he were seeing it for the first time and I could see the levers in his mind working.

"The answer to that is quite simple, Lieutenant," Mason said as if he were indulging a child. "We're not big drinkers and by 'finished' I meant that we had all had enough."

"Okay, Mr. Mason, you had had enough and you and Mr. Campion went to your rooms upstairs. How would you describe Mr. Braxton's mood when you left him?"

"Good. A good mood. We were all in a good mood. Perhaps a little sad that our vacation was ending but it had been a great two weeks…the weather…the fishing…the camaraderie."

"And what did Mr. Braxton say he was going to do when the two of you left him?"

Mason looked off in the distance as if he were trying to remember.

"As I recall, Lieutenant, David said he was going to sit and enjoy the fire and I guess he was really going to finish his drink and then heat our dinner."

He shifted his gaze back to me and I locked eyes with him.

"Mr. Mason, there wasn't any fire. The logs and kindling had been prepared but it was never lit."

Mason's color became noticeably paler and I saw a slight tic appear on his left cheek. He gave a forced laugh.

"I must have confused that last night with the other nights that we had a fire," he said.

"If everyone was in such a good mood and you usually had a fire, why didn't you light the prepared fire that night?" I asked in a low monotone.

The tic on his cheek turned into a twitching of his left eye and he was definitely nervous. A heavy silence followed my question and then, finally, he answered.

"I can't account for that. I thought we did."

I wanted to press him.

"So you and Mr. Campion left your best friend, the man you both had known intimately since childhood, sitting on the sofa, without a fire, and he was in a good mood and you all had had a great two weeks and everything was fine and in less than a half-hour he had shot himself…that's what you're telling me, right?"

His left eye-twitch was coming more rapidly and the corners of his mouth turned down and I thought he was on the verge of tears. Then he seemed to summon some inner strength and stood up but was still not looking at me.

"Yes, that's correct," he said with an air of finality.

"And you have no idea…no possible explanation…can offer no reason why David Braxton took his life?"

Mason's steely reserve was growing by the second.

"I'm afraid not." he said in a distinctly cold, even condescending, tone.

"The sheriff reported that you kept repeating the line, 'This shouldn't have happened.' What did you mean by that?"

"Just what anyone would mean by it," Mason said defiantly. "This was a tragedy that should never have occurred."

Mason glanced at his watch and started walking toward the stairs..

"I'm sorry but I have an important appointment, and if there are no further questions…"

"Not for now," I said, snapping my notebook shut. "But if I come up with any more, I know where I can find you." I returned his phony smile.

"Of course," Mason said, and the note of superiority he mustered in those two words made me want to smash his patrician nose. Instead, I thanked him and left. As soon as I reached the sidewalk outside Mason's townhouse I felt the craving for a cigarette. At a deli just two blocks away, I bought what I swore would be my last pack of Camels and lit up, sucking the smoke in greedily.

IX

I was getting an up-close look at how the rich and famous lived. When Peter Campion's mother, the Hollywood star Jessica Hunter, died about ten years earlier, she had, according to the newspaper accounts, parlayed several generous divorce settlements and some astute business investments into a significant fortune which was left entirely to her only child, Peter. Additionally, Peter's paternal grandmother, a Philadelphia society matron, had recently passed away, outliving Peter's father by more than fifteen years, and she, too, had left a sizeable chunk of her estate to her "beloved grandson, Peter."

The result of these legacies was clearly evident in Campion's home: a sprawling, full-floor apartment on Fifth Avenue where I was greeted by a doorman, a man in uniform behind a desk in the lobby who called up and announced me, and an elevator operator who whistled softly as he took me up to the twenty-second floor and let me out onto a private foyer where Campion was waiting for me.

Campion's face was, of course, very familiar to me since I saw it every morning over coffee as I watched a cable news channel where he was featured on several different programs. In person, however, his face appeared softer, less angular, and his height was impressive, at least six-foot-four. He was dressed casually in tan slacks and a white polo shirt, accentuating a lean body and muscular arms. He gave me a firm hand shake and a wide smile that instantly reminded me of his mother in all her sunny song-and-dance pictures of the fifties.

"Let's sit in the library," Campion said.

We walked along a long gallery whose walls were filled with large abstract paintings, and passed several rooms until Campion led me into a large room with massive book shelves, an unlit fireplace with an elaborately carved mantel and a spectacular view of Central Park. We sat across from each other on two brown leather sofas and Campion, looking relaxed and composed, waited for me to begin any conversation.

"Have you spoken to Jack Mason today?" I asked, hoping to catch him off guard. A wary look flashed across Campion's face and he hesitated before answering.

"Yes," he said, bringing his right foot up to rest on his left knee, still maintaining an air of casualness. His smile never vanished. "As a matter of fact, I just got off the phone with him a few minutes before you arrived"

"Then I guess he filled you in on everything," I said, trying to sound suspicious.

Campion betrayed no emotion.

"Jack and I talk at least twice a day since David's death. He's taking it very hard," he said impassively.

"And what about you?" I asked, just to gauge his response.

Campion looked directly at me and spoke in that well modulated baritone, as though he were delivering the latest news.

"David Braxton was my best friend since we were twelve," he said. "And Jack Mason, too. I will miss David for the rest of my life and I'm terribly sorry for what happened."

"What exactly did happen?" I asked, taking out my notebook.

"Surely you've heard all the details by now, Lieutenant, and must be tired of them," Campion said airily.

"Well, I'd like to hear them again, in your own words," I said assertively.

Sensing my determination, Campion recited all the events surrounding David Braxton's death, rattling them off as if he were reading them from a teleprompter. I was struck by how closely his recitation resembled Mason's version, down to the same words and phrases, with one exception. Campion said that he had "finished half" of his second drink and left the living room. Clearly, Mason had gone over every detail of my exchanges with him, and Campion was prepared.

"You said that you went upstairs to write a letter?" I asked.

"That's right," Campion said

"What stationery did you use?"

"Why, my own stationery," Campion replied calmly.

"You mean the stationery you left in your room at the lodge?"

Campion's eyes flickered but his voice remained calm.

"Yes, in the midst of everything else and our hasty departure, I left my stationery case there."

I flipped through my notes until I found what I was looking for.

"Why were you looking for writing paper in a desk at the Braxton lodge a few days earlier when you had your own?"

Campion hesitated and his brow furrowed slightly.

"Oh, that was just to scribble some notes on an idea I had for a documentary," he answered, breaking out with his mother's famous smile. It seemed forced.

"Do you have those notes?" I asked quickly.

Another hesitation, this time longer, and the smile was fading.

"No, I don't," he said, running his right hand through his curly blond hair, then crossing his arms on his chest. "I threw them away when I reread them on the trip home and decided not to pursue the idea."

"Where?" I asked.

"Where what?" he said, his voice rising slightly.

"Where did you throw them away?"

I watched Campion's eyes dart toward the ceiling

"At the airport," he said.

"Which airport?" I asked quickly

"The one in Idaho," he replied.

"But didn't you fly back in Senator Braxton's private plane?" I asked, leaning forward and staring at Campion.

"Yes, yes, of course," he said, seeing why I might question this detail. "But when we got to the airport, there was a slight delay because they were still fueling the plane, so I sat down and wanted to get my mind off of everything that had happened, so I read my notes on the documentary I was thinking about doing. It seemed the best way to…"

"How long was the delay?" I interrupted him.

"A good half hour, as I recall," Campion said.

I made a notation in my notebook to check with the pilot of Senator Braxton's plane as Campion looked on, and now I could sense that he was nervous.

"What was the documentary about?" I asked casually, and now Campion's composure was starting to visibly crack.

"About the endless Israeli-Palestinian conflict," he said as though thinking out loud as he reorganized his body on the sofa.

"Hasn't there been a number of programs on that very subject on your own station?" I asked, taking a shot in the dark. "What was your new angle?"

Campion waved his right hand dismissively. "Nothing much, really," he said, trying to sound casual. "Just about the refugees' struggles to survive and start new lives in different locations."

"Sounds pretty much like what I've seen," I said, pushing the envelope.

"That's why I threw the idea out," Campion said, now clearly annoyed.

I changed the subject.

"Mr. Campion, describe for me how you handled the gun in the desk drawer at the lodge"

"Well, I moved it aside," he said, clearly prepared for this topic.

"Yes," I said, "but please describe exactly how you moved it aside."

Campion's smile had long since left his face and his eyelids lowered in a scornful look.

"I can't really say," he said. "I just moved it!"

"And is that how your thumbprint appeared on the gun, next to David Braxton's prints?" I was supplying him with answers, hoping he might think I believed everything he said.

"Yes, that's right."

"You didn't pick up the gun?"

"Not that I can remember," Campion said.

"And that was the only time you touched it?"

"Yes, the only time."

Now I sprung the trap.

"Would you be willing to take a polygraph test, Mr. Campion?"

The expression on his face changed completely and somehow, although he looked nothing like Jack Mason, his expression seemed identical to Mason's at the end of my interview with him: defensive, arrogant and condescending.

"Look here, Lieutenant Russo," he said, leaving forward, "just what are you driving at?"

"I honestly don't know, Mr. Campion," I admitted. "Senator Braxton doesn't think his son committed suicide and, frankly, neither do I."

Campion's eyes grew larger at my last assertion but his gaze remained steady.

"Then what exactly do you think happened?" he asked, indignation washing over his face.

"I don't know…but I aim to find out."

We sat in silence as Campion leaned back into the sofa and flung his left arm across its back.

"You really can't be serious," he said, affecting a look of incredulity.

"I'm very serious," I shot back.

He shook his head in disbelief and stood up.

"If that's your position, then I'm afraid our interview is over," he said, turning toward the library door.

"Why did you call your lawyer before you called the sheriff," I asked quickly

"That's just a reflexive action for a man in my position," he said, a note of pomposity creeping into his voice.

"And why did you call your philosophy professor at Yale?"

"Because Jack and I were devastated by what had happened and we were clutching at straws and needed to talk to someone we could trust."

It flashed across my brain that his words were almost identical to Mason's, including the "clutching at straws" and "someone we could trust."

Campion was walking toward the library door and my next question was aimed at his back.

"You both called your wives," I said. "Don't you trust them?"

He stopped, turned and gave me a withering look.

"You don't understand," he said, now clearly angry, "and I'm afraid that's all I'm prepared to say."

Silently, Campion led the way down the long gallery to the elevator and I followed him.

"You really think David Braxton committed suicide?" I asked as we crossed the marble foyer towards the door of the elevator.

Campion turned and glared at me.

"Of course I do. I was there!"

"But you can offer no reason or logical explanation for this tragic turn in his life. There was no clue in those final days…nothing said or hinted at …no shift in his personality for you, as his long-time best friend, to become alarmed?"

Campion didn't bother to look at me but continued striding toward the elevator as he threw a terse "No" over his shoulder. I was clearly being stonewalled.

He turned toward me as the elevator door opened and shot me a phony smile, the kind he gave automatically at the end of one of his TV broadcasts.

"Goodbye, Lieutenant Russo."

The elevator operator was smiling, too, as I stepped in and the door closed. I wanted to punch someone, something, anything. I also wanted a cigarette.

X

I went downtown to my office and had a brief chat with my Captain about other cases I had been involved with before the Braxton case became my primary focus.

The public has this notion that, like Sherlock Holmes and the Royal Canadian Mounties, we always get our man. This is a helpful myth for the police to keep alive. I'm sure it's reinforced by all the cop shows on television where, in the course of an hour, every criminal is brought to justice and every case is solved.

The truth is quite different, especially with murders. You get a few transparent cases like a jealous husband who finds his wife in bed with some guy and kills both of them with his hunting rifle and then tries to make it look like a break-in and robbery gone bad. With a good detective interrogating him, it takes a very short time before the husband confesses.

Most murder cases are more challenging and a few are downright baffling. Cases can go unsolved for years until some anonymous caller gives us a tip that leads us in a whole new direction. Sometimes the killer, after years of fighting his conscience, finally gives up and confesses. Sometimes a detective reviews all the evidence for the twentieth time and suddenly sees something that everyone overlooked.

The point to stress here is that detective work is slow, laborious, often tedious and frustrating. A detective needs patience and persistence and an occasional bit of luck in order to perform his job well.

I was not surprised to learn from my captain that there was nothing new on my other cases. On my desk I found a fax from Tom Corrigan.

George, I finally got a chance to speak to Anna Jenkowski, the housekeeper. She had left on Wednesday, the day of Braxton's death, to attend the funeral of an uncle in St. Louis and returned yesterday. She wasn't there to witness anything but she did say to me that every year she noticed that the three men always arrived in very high spirits and then in the last days of their stay seemed to grow tense and serious. Now, I know this could be because their vacation was coming to an end, but Mrs. Jenkowski stressed the total change in mood so I thought I'd pass it along. Just something else to include in your puzzle, Detective Lieutenant, big-shot city sleuth! Please keep me in the loop. Lily and Keith both send their regards. Tom

XI

Since it was lunchtime, I went over to Skelly's, the local hangout for cops and detectives, and met some of my buddies. We had a few beers and I couldn't keep taking cigarettes from them so I bought a pack of my own, but this, I told myself, was definitely my last. On my way back from the cigarette machine I spotted John O'Shea, a detective from my squad, who was sitting in a booth with a couple of guys I didn't recognize. O'Shea waved to me and called out, "Hey, Russo, did you hear that Theresa broke up with her boyfriend? Now's your chance before the sharks move in." He gave me a wink and a broad smile and I nodded but didn't smile back.

The detectives in my squad room gave me only about three months of mourning for Ginny before they were trying to fix me up. Sisters, cousins, neighbors' daughters, old girlfriends—every female, single, divorced or widowed between twenty-five and fifty—were suggested to me as the next possible Mrs. George Russo. I figured I was not much of a catch, with one failed marriage and one that had been very happy but ended after only three years. And even after a year since Ginny's death, she still haunted my days and nights like a song that keeps playing over and over in your head and you just can't stop hearing it.

When I grabbed my first cup of coffee in the morning, still half asleep and totally unfocused, I thought of the ritual Ginny made of our having coffee together to start the day and be reconnected after our lovemaking and sleep of the night before. Whenever I was talking to a woman, any woman, I thought of the way that Ginny listened intently to anything I shared with her. Her beautiful brown eyes gazing directly at me and her head cocked a little to the side, she would murmur little sounds or shake her head or raise her eyebrows or frown or smile to express her reactions without interrupting me. When I was with my kids, I thought of how patient she was with George Jr. who, in his muddled thirteen-year-old brain thought Ginny was the cause of my breakup with his mother, even though I told him that I hadn't met Ginny until almost a year after our separation.

Carolyn and I had wrangled over the terms of our divorce for nearly a year until finally we agreed on a settlement. I had taken out a loan to give her half the market value of our house in Queens as part of the agreement so that I could keep the house and my kids would have a familiar place to come to for their visits with me. Familiarity was all I could offer them after our divorce. Carolyn was now living in a big house on over an acre of land in Great Neck, Long Island with her new husband—she remarried even quicker than I did—and they had a pool and a tennis court.

As fate would have it, Ginny was the loan officer who handled my loan. Vivacious, funny, intelligent and damn pretty, she caught my attention right away and in our brief exchanges I learned that she wasn't married. When she called me to say I could come in and get my loan, I figured this would be the last time I'd probably see her.

"How about celebrating with me over dinner?" I remember asking her, and her response was strong and instantaneous: "Yes, I'd love to!"

That night, in a small Italian restaurant where the flickering candle on the table made her look really beautiful, I learned that she was eight years younger than me, had been engaged for nearly three years but never married, had lost her mother to cancer when she was only fifteen, leaving her the care giver to her father and younger brother. She had worked her way through St. John's University on Long Island and had held her present job with the bank for the last three years.

For every fact I learned about Ginny, she learned about six more from me, gently prodding me with questions and listening attentively. I'm not by nature a talkative guy, as my first wife would gladly attest, but there was something in the way she asked her questions—a low, soothing voice, an alert, ready smile, eyes focused intently on me—that made me open up like a kid in the confessional.

By the end of the evening the sparks were flying but I didn't want to rush things. After our fourth date she suggested we spend the weekend together. That was the most exciting, satisfying, joyful weekend of my life. We both knew this was the real thing and we were married four months after the day of our first date.

Any other woman would probably have objected to living in the house that the first wife had called home, but not Ginny. She just moved in and made it her own. I still have the house and can't part with it because it represents the history of my adult life, both good and bad. Ginny kept working but eased into my life as if she'd always been a part of it.

I'm not saying that she was perfect. We both gladly accepted the other's foibles as part of the package. She drank milk out of the carton like a kid; she left drawers open in the kitchen and she even snored a little, but my state of happiness with her was complete. I didn't want any more kids and I knew that she agreed only reluctantly, and if she had been spared to me I think we probably would have had a baby because we both wanted to make the other person happy in every possible way.

I was with her when the doctor gave her the news of her cancer and how it had spread so quickly. As I sat beside her, listening to his words, the bottom fell out of my life. At one point she grabbed my arm and winced in pain because I was so goddamn angry at this lousy spin of the life-wheel that I was unconsciously squeezing her hand with a lot of force. But our time together from that day forward, just five short months to the day she died, was even more intense and joyous than it had been up to the day of the news. The way she faced death, with so much bravery and thoughtfulness for others, made me love and admire her more.

My kids saw how totally preoccupied I was with making every moment with Ginny count and they cut me lots of slack during those few short months. My two girls had quickly and totally succumbed to Ginny's casual, loving ways without feeling they were betraying their mother—a compromise that my son could never make, although in Ginny's last month even he made small gestures of reconciliation, which pleased Ginny so much.

One day she was there, still clinging to life and I held her hand, probably squeezing too hard again as I tried to force life back into her wasting body, and the next day she was gone. Of course it was then that I discovered that she hadn't left me, and the haunting began. I was still with her, still sharing our morning coffee, still looking for her when I came home from work, still discussing my kids with her, still making love to her at night.

Lots of work only relieved my preoccupation with Ginny temporarily, and after three months, when my fellow detectives must have thought I was just mopping around, looking like a sad-eyed hound dog, they decided it was time to start looking to the future instead of dwelling in the past. They bombarded me with candidates for George Russo's next happy chapter, be it only a one-night stand, a brief romance or another walk down the aisle. The trouble was, I wasn't ready. As hard as they pushed women on me, the harder I pushed back, taking no initiative to call sweet Helen or smart Monica or fun-loving Stacy or the sexy Diana. I guess the guys finally realized that I needed more time and pretty much left me alone.

Never having experienced such a deep sense of loss before, I had no idea how long this empty feeling would last, although I had heard about the different stages of grief. Ginny never left my heart but she gradually receded from my every waking thought. Then, like a new moon rising, old stirrings for sex and intimacy and companionship led me once again to think about my future.

I was forty-six years old; my kids would be all grown up in a few more years and I certainly didn't want to spend the rest of my life alone. I wasn't too sure about another marriage but I was sure that I wanted to be in a committed relationship, sharing my life with someone. Still, I didn't give any indication to my squad buddies that I was again on the dating market because I didn't want their well-meaning but mostly inappropriate barrage of candidates.

When John O'Shea called out to me about Theresa, that was different. O'Shea and I had been in high school together and played on the varsity basketball team. Theresa Costello was a cheerleader for our team. She was my date to the senior prom, my steady girlfriend throughout my senior year, and the first girl I had sex with—I'm not talking about making out or copping a feel or lots of soul kissing which had been the extent of my sexual repertoire, along with raunchy fantasies and self abuse, from seventh grade through my junior year.

Theresa and I, by mutual agreement, went all the way the night of our senior prom, under the boardwalk in Long Beach,

Long Island at four in the morning, my heroic grunting and groaning drowned out by the gently lapping waves. I can't say it was the most satisfying or romantic experience I've ever had, especially when the sand invaded our blanket and then our bodies in the most inconvenient places. It was more the pride I felt in knowing I could do it and knowing that I had done it satisfactorily, according to Theresa, and now I was not only graduating from high school but was also promoting myself to full manhood. For the rest of my life, I couldn't hear the song, Under the Boardwalk, without thinking of Theresa and Long Beach and sand and sex.

You never forget your first love and the first girl you go all the way with, and Theresa was both. She was smart and flip and full of fun and everyone liked her. She was considered a beauty by her classmates, primarily for her beautiful red hair and large green eyes and great smile, and especially for her big boobs and long legs.

Every testosterone-driven adolescent in my school was obsessed with girls' breasts. Girls with little personality or looks could still be popular if they had large breasts and wore sweaters that accentuated them. Theresa was popular for her personality and sharp sense of humor as well as for her looks, but, somehow, in some indefinable rule of adolescent partnering, her having big melons certified my reputation as a stud.

Shortly after graduation, Theresa's family moved to Seattle, Washington, and despite our fervent vows of continuing our relationship, after a few short months of exchanging letters—I hated to write and felt compelled to say flowery things I didn't mean—our long-distance romance fizzled, I think pretty much by mutual boredom.

I started working full-time in my Uncle Joe's hardware store in Flushing and going to Queensborough Community College at night, but in 1968, because I wasn't a full-time college student—couldn't afford to be—I was drafted and sent off to Vietnam.

Every foot soldier who's seen action in any war, comes home a changed man, and I was no exception. While I didn't perform any heroic deeds, preferring to keep my ass as safe as possible, I could honestly say that I had never shirked my duty and had been tested in many ways: unbearable heat and fungus infections constantly attacking your body; endless maneuvers searching for the enemy in steaming jungles filled with all kinds of things, besides the enemy, that could kill you; seeing one man from my platoon die instantly from a sniper's bullet just a few feet away from me, a moment after I had handed him one of my cigarettes; and witnessing a rotating number of wounded men being air lifted back to base camp on stretchers.

Any soldier in a battle zone becomes an intimate friend of death. You don't talk about death; you don't write home about death; you try not to think about death. But somewhere deep inside you, death is present in a most intimate and immediate way. It greets you in the morning and hovers by your side all day, and when you finally close your eyes at night you defiantly give it the finger for escaping its clutches that day. But living so closely with the possibility of death at any moment makes you value life all the more, every second of it

When you've tasted, touched and felt death and come to value life more fully in such a living hell, and then you eventually escape with your body miraculously unscathed and your mind filled with haunting memories that still don't cripple you, you never look at life quite the same again. You're grateful to God or fate or luck when you think of all your fellow soldiers who came home with permanent physical or mental impairments, or didn't come home at all.

You thrive on a return to normalcy and consciously relish the little, ordinary things of day-to-day living, at least for a time, until the war memories recede and your resolutions to live more fully, more appreciatively, recede with them. Still, the imprint of deadly combat never fully leaves you and, in some indefinable way, separates you from those who have never experienced first-hand the realities of war, the transformation of decent, ordinary men into killing machines and the daily combat within yourself to conquer fear and stay sane.

So it was with me.

I wondered if David Braxton had felt some of the same things I did, since he had evidently seen a lot of action as an officer in Nam and had received a slew of medals. He had also been wounded but, judging from the very active life he had led since then, he clearly had fully recovered. How vastly different our lives had been since Nam, I thought.

When I returned home two years later, I took the test for the New York City Police Department and was accepted. That's when I met John O'Shea again—we were in the same class at the Police Academy—and he told me that he had heard through his sister that Theresa had gotten married. Her parents were back in our old neighborhood, never having sold their house, just renting it, but Theresa had stayed in Seattle with her husband.

By that time I had met Carolyn on a double date and we hit it off and started seeing a lot of each other. We got engaged about a year after that but she kept putting off the date of our wedding. I only learned years later, again from John O'Shea's sister, that the reason for the delay was because Carolyn was also seeing the guy who would become her second husband At that time he didn't want to get married so she settled for me, and we were finally married in 1973. My oldest daughter, Emily, was born in '75, and then in '78 we had my son, George Jr., and my youngest, adorable Beth, arrived in '81.

There was always something missing from our marriage; some underlying layer of discontent that we never spoke about and never confronted—it was just there, quietly waiting to gather strength and come charging out. My wife had champagne tastes and I could only offer her beer. As Carolyn became more immersed in her romantic dreams of upward mobility, glamour and excitement, and saw that her poor slob of a husband, a bona fide working class stiff, lacked all the qualities or interests necessary to facilitate her climb, her resentment rushed out and loomed over our home like an ever pending storm.

Sarcasm became my wife's attack mode. She saved her special darts for social occasions with friends and neighbors and unleashed them at me in withering tones after she had a few drinks. I didn't fight back, which made her all the more furious, but by that time I didn't give a damn for her or our marriage. I stayed around only for the kids. Then her original heartthrob came back into the picture, rich and paunchy, and this time around he was ready for marriage, so she bolted.

John O'Shea kept me informed about Theresa, thanks to the endless stream of gossip and news that came from his sister. Theresa had divorced her husband and moved back to her parents' home for a short while before moving out when she took up with some guy from the old neighborhood whom I didn't know. They had a long-term relationship but never got married, and she never had any kids. And now O'Shea was alerting me to Theresa's being unattached again. Before leaving the bar I dropped by his table and asked for her phone number.

"You can reach her at her parents' house on Elm Street. They're in the book," O'Shea said with a big smile that I swear was almost a leer, but I just said, "Thanks," and walked out.

XII

Continuing my private tour of the homes of the rich and famous, the next morning I found myself in a mammoth loft in the East Village where David Braxton and his celebrated wife, Nadira, lived with their three children. A former warehouse district, this area had been recently gentrified by millionaires who wanted something different from the usual opulent apartments on the Upper East Side and along the famous avenues like Park and Fifth. Even John F. Kennedy Jr. had chosen a loft, so different from his mother's elegant Fifth Avenue apartment overlooking Central Park.

With no doorman or other attendants to greet me or announce me; I rang the apartment number I was given by Nadira when I arranged this meeting—no names were on the outside directory, just numbers. A voice came on the intercom and I immediately recognized it as one of the most well known voices in the world.

"Who is it please?" the throaty voice asked, sending tingles up my spine.

"Detective Lieutenant Russo, Mrs. Braxton," I boldly answered.

"Oh, yes," she said and I was buzzed in.

A self-service elevator took me to the fourth floor where I stepped into a small foyer. The one visible door was opened and there she stood, the supermodel who had been a part of more of my fantasies than just about anyone else, including my two wives. Since we were both around six feet tall and she was wearing flats, I stared directly into her huge brown eyes, thinking of how, for years, they had stared at me from hundreds of magazine covers on newsstands that I passed every day before she married David Braxton.

I crossed the distance between the elevator and the door in just a few steps and took her extended hand. Her handshake was surprisingly firm. Immediately, I was sucked into her extraordinary beauty. Even with her hair casually pulled back in a thick ponytail, she took my breath away. Her thin straight nose, the full lips and flawless, pale complexion were set off by high cheekbones, a strong jaw line and a wide forehead. Her eyes were magnetic, drawing you in with a dark iris flecked with gold and accentuated with thick dark lashes and thin arched brows. I was conscious of never having been this close to a really beautiful woman and my instinct was to stand still and drink in every detail She gave me a small smile.

"Come in, Lieutenant Russo," she said, turning away from the door and walking into the apartment. She was wearing a beige sweater over charcoal slacks and as I followed her into the apartment I took in the curves beneath the fabric that had graced the annual swimsuit cover of Sports Illustrated more than any other model. I started to feel like a dog in heat and cautioned myself to rein in my fantasies.

When I finally took my eyes off of her, I saw that we were standing in a huge space with a ceiling at least twenty feet high and a spiral staircase leading to a mezzanine area where I guessed the bedrooms were. The kitchen was done entirely in steel and was separated from the living, dining and media areas only by a long stainless steel bar. The main room was at least fifty feet long and twenty feet wide and it reminded me of the living room at Senator Braxton's Idaho lodge. Here, too, the space was divided only by furniture groupings, and high above us I glimpsed the industrial pipes running across the ceiling and extending down walls, all part of the popular loft look.

I couldn't help but reflect on how hard my parents had struggled to get out of a Brooklyn tenement apartment with exposed pipes and to migrate to Queens, then considered a suburb, for a three-bedroom, one-bath attached house with a thirty-by-twenty-foot back yard, all of which they considered Paradise. And now here were the rich folk returning to run-down neighborhoods and making exposed pipes and old brick walls and concrete floors chic. That's the power of money, I thought. What's next? Living in teepees? Wherever the rich trendsetters led, the masses would follow, I was sure. I called it Russo's Trickle-Down Law of Socio-

Economic Aspirations, which was okay with me since that's what made our economy grow and kept our country strong. But it did tickle me when I observed how idolatrous the middle-class was in slavishly imitating the rich to feed their own need for upward mobility and expanding status. My brief reverie was interrupted by that low, sultry voice—like Ava Gardner's, I thought, and the tingles returned.

"Would you like some coffee?" my goddess, taking a seat on a long, modern sectional sofa, asked me.

"No thanks," I replied, sitting on a chair opposite her, separated by a large ebony coffee table displaying several small, hand-carved African statues, a large steel ashtray and a thick file folder.

Nadira took a cigarette from a carved wooden box on the coffee table and pointed it at me.

"Do you mind?" she asked, and I waved my hand vigorously, so grateful to be able to give my permission for her to do anything. If she had asked to carve her initials on my forehead, I probably would have eagerly mumbled yes.

"Would you like one?" she asked, clearly an afterthought, and although I had given up smoking for the seventy-seventh time the day before, the thought of smoking with this gorgeous woman suggested a shared intimacy that I couldn't resist. I eagerly took a cigarette from the box she held out to me and then she picked up a small carved statue and flipped its head back to reveal a lighter. She pushed its extended arm down and held out the light for me. I leaned forward and touched her hand to steady the lighter but my own hand was trembling with electric delight and, to add to my sensual overload, I picked up a slight whiff of her subtle perfume

We both sat back and inhaled, and the smoke felt good as it reunited with my lungs and traveled back out through my nostrils. She didn't seem to inhale and quickly let the smoke curl around her tongue before exhaling through her open mouth, turning her head to the side and starting me down the road to fantasy land again. Calling on all my professional reserve, I placed my cigarette on the large silver ashtray on the coffee table before taking out my notebook. Nadira watched my actions through unfocused eyes, appearing tense and distracted.

"First, let me say I'm sorry for your loss, Mrs. Braxton," I said in as sympathetic a tone as I could muster. "I lost my wife to cancer a year ago and it was unexpected."

Nadira nodded her head slightly and a misty film crept into the corners of her eyes but she said nothing.

"I know how painful this must be for you, but can you think of any reason why your husband would take his life?"

She gazed off into space and then a few tears spilled across her cheeks and she shook her head no. My instant impulse was to be her hero and rush over to her and cradle her in my arms and rub her back and say soothing things while she sobbed quietly against my chest. Fortunately, I kept this impulse in check and reluctantly asked another question.

"Were there any health issues, or financial issues or…" here I hesitated but felt forced to say it, "marital problems that might have a bearing on your husband's state of mind?"

"None," she said, staring at me with those beautiful eyes, glistening with tears, and I again wanted to take her in my arms and comfort her. She stamped out her cigarette in the steel ashtray and began to speak, looking off in the distance again.

"Ever since I heard the news, I've been racking my brain trying to make some sense of it, but I can't. I can't! If you knew my husband, Lieutenant, you'd know why this is the most unbelievable thing that could ever happen."

She paused and reached for another cigarette. I rushed to grab the lighter and extend my arm across the coffee table toward her, hoping fervently that she'd touch my hand as she lit up. But she just lowered her face to meet the light and I was as disappointed as a kid being passed over for a birthday party. The tear stains on her cheeks showed no trace of smeared make-up, so that flawless complexion was truly hers, I concluded. No wonder during her modeling years she had been seen constantly on television ads for cosmetics, facial creams, rejuvenating lotions and skin care products.

I flashed back to my first wife's addiction to the facial products that Nadira sold on TV and chuckled to myself how duped my wife had been, thinking that the creams would turn her blotchy complexion into the luminous skin Nadira showed in the

75

commercials, when all along it wasn't the product but the perfect skin underneath the product.

Nadira leaned forward and bathed me with her lush dark eyes.

"No one loved life more than my husband and no one had more to live for! From the first day I met him 'til the day he left for Idaho…" She paused, struggling to hold on to her composure, "he was the happiest, the most alive, the most exciting man I had ever known. He usually only slept about six hours a night because he used to say that life offered too many wonderful possibilities to be wasted in sleep. He treated every day like a great adventure and said that no day should be wasted. He was always thinking of new things to try: skydiving, parasailing, rock climbing, even boogie boarding. He encouraged our kids to meet challenges and try new things—musical instruments, new sports, different hobbies, languages, painting, creative writing, dancing, karate—anything that might expand their horizons. He was a terrific father, loving and playful and supportive, who always found time for his kids, and he filled our lives with joy and zest and love and …"

She stopped, placing her cigarette in the steel ashtray and then covered her face with her hands as her shoulders gently shook. I sat in motionless silence, thinking how David Braxton must have been one hell of a guy to make this extraordinary creature grieve for him so deeply. I loved my second wife, Ginny, completely and mindlessly and I found the strength to comfort her through the months of her fight with cancer and speedy decline. I cried unashamedly when she died, although my deep sense of personal despair was mixed with relief that her inevitable end had come mercifully quickly. I missed her when she was gone like I would miss my arms or my legs if they were taken away from me, because my being was totally meshed with hers.

The void Ginny left in my life was, for a time, all enveloping, and now I sat in this huge loft and looked across the coffee table at the most gorgeous woman I had ever seen up close in real life and I knew instinctively that the loss of her husband was felt as greatly as my losing Ginny. At least mine was the natural culmination of unfortunate events, as the cancer took its inevitable course, but Nadira's loss was far more jolting, more shocking, more horrendous in its unfathomable circumstances for which she clearly had no satisfactory answers and only endless, torturous questions.

As if to relieve the intense sympathy I felt for this woman's unbearable sadness, my mind turned in a quirky direction and I suddenly thought that if I died, my first wife would throw a party and maybe even have the guests play a new game called "Pin the Badge on the Detective."

Nadira pulled out a handkerchief from a pocket in her slacks and wiped her eyes.

"I'm sorry," was all she said, delicately blowing her beautiful nose.

"I understand," was all I replied, struggling once again to keep my unprofessional comforting impulses in check.

Our intimacy was interrupted by the ringing of her cell phone which she extracted from another pocket in her slacks. A brief conversation ensued before she said goodbye and put the phone on the coffee table.

"Last minute arrangements for the memorial service," she explained.

"When is it?" I asked.

"Tomorrow afternoon at two... The Hundred Club."

That triggered another thought.

"Did you know Professor Jenkins?" I asked gently.

She looked puzzled, as if running the name through a long mental rolodex, and then seemed to find the person who went with the name.

"Oh, David's favorite philosophy professor from Yale! Yes, I met him at our wedding reception."

"No other time?"

"No," she said, staring off as if recollecting her thoughts. "He was quite ill a few years ago and David and Peter and Jack all went up to see him in New Haven, and David spoke to him on the phone quite often, but I never saw him after our wedding."

Now I asked a loaded question.

"I know that your husband and Peter Campion and Jack Mason were very close friends," I said, "but was there ever any friction among them that you're aware of?."

"Never!" she said quickly, shaking her head from side to side, and new tears glistened in her eyes. "They were like brothers. Jack's wife, Deirdre, used to say that they loved one another more than they loved us, but I knew that wasn't true. There was just this great bond between the three of them…a loving affinity…a sharing of their love for life. All three of them were so high on life! I always thought they shared some secret gift for living, for extracting the most from every day, every moment. Even though they had all accomplished so much, sometimes they were like three kids who competed with each other, like when Peter got his pilot's license and Jack and David had to get theirs too, or when Jack achieved the highest level in Tae Kwon Do and, of course, David and Peter had to follow suit. I guess it goes back to their years at Yale when they all competed and graduated the top three in their class. They seemed to use their competitive spirit to spur them on to more accomplishments but it never interfered with their friendship. Their laughter was infectious; they were never down. The three of them in a room together was like watching a three-ring circus. The wives could barely keep up with them, they were so charged with energy and always looking for fun and adventure, but so loving at the same time. Really, you should have seen them together; they laughed and joked and ribbed one another and were spectacular fun."

She stopped and looked embarrassed as if she had been overheard in a private reverie. I gave her a big, reassuring smile.

"And you and the other two wives didn't resent this close friendship or their going off on their annual trip to Idaho?"

Nadira cocked her head as I marveled at her long, creamy neck.

"Not at all!" she said emphatically. "Deirdre Mason used to say it gave us a chance to recharge our batteries because life with our husbands was always full-out." She paused. "Maybe Margaret Campion was a wee bit jealous, but even so, she never really said anything negative—it was just a feeling I picked up."

She reached for another cigarette. She was either a chain smoker or her nerves were frayed. I hurried to pick up the camouflaged lighter and light her cigarette. Her long fingers and beautifully shaped nails briefly touched my extended hand this time and I felt those shivers of excitement down my spine.

"How could we resent their friendship when they were all loving and devoted husbands and added such pleasure to one another's lives!" she exclaimed, as smoke circled in her mouth.

"From everything you've told me, Mrs. Braxton," I said, rising from my chair, "there's no reason, no motivation for your husband to have taken his life, but there has to be some reason why he did."

"I don't believe that!" she snapped, color rising in her cheeks and spreading across her pale skin, and I could feel her anger and her anguish.

"Honestly, I don't believe it either," I said, and her face softened immediately, "but we've got to find out what really happened."

Then, reluctantly, I hit her with another hard question.

"You've just spoken glowingly about Mr. Campion and Mr. Mason and how close they were to your husband, but remember that they're saying he committed suicide, and they were the only ones there when he died. How do you account for that?"

I watched her beautiful face contort with conflicting emotions.

"I can't," she said, in a barely audible voice, tears again rising in her eyes, "but there has to be some other explanation! There just has to be!"

She sat there, looking off into space through tear-filled eyes, like some wounded animal, and I yearned to be her knight in shining armor who rode to the rescue of this beautiful woman in distress, but I suppressed this wild impulse and tried to console her within the bounds of my professional role.

"Mrs. Braxton, I give you my promise that I will do everything I can to find the truth."

She gazed at me with a pitiful look that I couldn't make out if it was doubt or gratitude, so I smiled reassuringly. She dabbed at her eyes.

"I'd like to show you something," she said, and she rose from the sofa and headed for the spiral staircase. I watched her elegant figure ascending the staircase and disappear, then descend a few minutes later, holding an envelope in her hand. She came toward me and handed me the envelope. Her hands were trembling and her voice was low.

"This letter was delivered to me yesterday by John Calverton, David's lawyer. He was instructed by David to give it to me if anything should ever happen to David and I survived him. Evidently, David had written this shortly after we were married, before the birth of our first child, and he entrusted it to his personal lawyer. Read it, Lieutenant!"

I sat down again and extracted two sheets of paper with David Braxton's name embossed on the top of each page. I read.

My dearest Nadie,

As we await the birth of our first child, my heart is bursting with joy and love for you and our baby. Each morning I like to wake up before you do so I can gaze at your beautiful face and remind myself how lucky I am to have found the most beautiful girl in the world who is beautiful not just in face and form but in every way. You are my partner in life, my soul mate, my inspiration, and you will be a magnificent mother. Thank you my darling for blessing me with your love, for giving yourself so completely to me, for joining in with my exuberant pleasures and making yourself and our home the center, the bedrock of my life. With everything that I have been given, my greatest challenge has been to waste nothing, not time or riches or talents or love but to utilize my gifts and endowments to explore life at a heightened level of intensity, as if each day were my last. I want you to know that if anything unforeseen should ever happen to me, I have lived each day to the fullest and consider your love to be the greatest gift of my happy life.

It was signed, *"Your adoring and grateful husband, David"*

I read the letter twice while Nadira stood by my chair.

"Does that sound like a man who would take his own life?" she asked defiantly as I replaced the pages in the envelope and handed the letter back to her.

"No , it doesn't," I said, rising from my chair.

What I didn't say was how I was struck by the ominous tone of what was supposed to be a love letter on such a forthcoming happy occasion. David Braxton must have been all of thirty-five years old when he wrote that letter, since his oldest child was now nine, so why would he even think about "anything unforeseen"?

I thought about death a lot in Nam and after I became a cop and a friend who had gone through the Police Academy with me got killed during a drug bust. I thought about it a lot more when Ginny was dying, but those weren't any of the circumstances that David Braxton faced. His mother and father and three younger siblings were all living and thriving, according to my reading up on the family. So what the hell pushed a guy, known for his great zest for life, to think such dark thoughts at such a young age and on such a happy occasion as the coming birth of his first child? And why hadn't he given the letter to his wife instead of giving it to his lawyer with instructions that it should be delivered to her after his death?

I felt very frustrated. What made this guy tick? I couldn't get into his head. Was that because he was so different from me? Besides his being rich and famous, I recognized that he was brilliant; being valedictorian of his Yale class proved that. And he had been a philosophy major so I guessed that called for a lot of deep thinking. Philosophy was a subject totally alien to me. My father had the "philosophy" of doing onto others before you let them do anything to you. As a kid, when I heard my mother saying that every challenge could be viewed as an obstacle or an opportunity, was she expressing a philosophy or a positive mental attitude?

After all my years as a cop and everything I had seen, as well as my failed marriage, I probably had the philosophy that life is short and hard and then you die. I heard people say that their philosophy was to live and let live. But this, I knew, was just a common "street philosophy," mere catch phrases, and not some systematic study of the great thinkers of different periods, the real "philosophers." How had that shaped his thinking beyond his reference to living each day to the fullest, which any television commercial for pantyhose or hair conditioner was now using as a sales gimmick? That idea to get the most out of life was being thrown about in our culture so superficially that it was trite and meaningless. Yet it obviously meant something else to David

Braxton. And he did seem to get the most out of his life, including taking some risky physical chances, right up to the day he turned around and supposedly ended it. No wonder his loved ones couldn't believe such a turnaround, even in the face of some pretty convincing evidence.

"Did your husband ever talk about philosophy, Mrs. Braxton?"

Nadira gave me a blank stare.

"What I means is, did he ever say what philosopher's thoughts most heavily influenced his thinking regarding his own life."

A light of recognition came into those beautiful eyes.

"Lieutenant, my husband didn't so much talk philosophy as live it. Of course he read philosophers. It was a lifetime pursuit. He spoke four other languages, you know—German, French, Spanish and Russian, and he knew Greek and Latin—so he could read many of the great philosophers in the original text."

Nadira paused when she saw a look of astonishment pass over my face, as I reacted to this latest piece of biographical news. When writing papers in college or writing reports as a cop or a detective, I struggled enough with my native English and never felt I had a sure command and was always checking reference books. And in school when we had to read any classic work dating back to before the twentieth century, with the long, long sentences and all the words no one ever used anymore, I was good for three paragraphs before dozing off or flinging the book across the room in frustration and thereafter using the Cliff Notes to get a passing grade. And here was this guy speaking five languages and reading in seven. He really did live life, physically and mentally, on a different level. It was almost like we came from different species. My admiration for him soared but my confusion only deepened.

Nadira continued. "David would occasionally make a reference to some philosopher, or quote a poem or a book that he greatly admired, but he was never a showoff about his vast knowledge. I'm sure he probably had discussions with Peter and Jack, but that was their world and I felt no need to intrude on it, any more than he did on my world of fashion. But surely his entire life was the acting out of his philosophy: his tremendous zest for life; his endless curiosity and boundless enthusiasm; his great love of adventure and passion for the arts; his caring and giving nature; his loving relationships with so many people; his great generosity of spirit."

She stopped, as if suddenly self-conscious of listing all her husband's virtues to a stranger, and I could sense that she might start to cry again, so I abruptly changed the subject.

"Do you mind if I attend your husband's memorial service?" I asked.

"No, but why would you want to do that?" she asked, looking puzzled.

"I'd just like to observe everybody in Mr. Braxton's immediate circle," I answered.

"It's a private service," she said, "but I'll leave your name at the desk. Do you know where The Hundred Club is?"

"Yes," I said, not really sure.

Our interview was over. Nadira walked me to the door of the apartment and again shook hands with me.

"Tomorrow, 2 P.M.," she reminded me.

The door closed on that mesmerizing, beautiful face, made all the more haunting by the overcast shadows of the deepest grief. As I descended in the self-service elevator I felt I was leaving a realm inhabited by, if not gods and goddesses, certainly people who didn't inhabit my ordinary world. It was a humbling experience.

XIII

Back at my office I put in a call to the office of Senator Braxton on his private line. His secretary answered and put me through to him right away.

"Have you anything to report?" he asked me, cutting to the chase.

"Not yet—just a lot of loose ends," I admitted, and there was a silence at the other end. "I do have a question for you, Senator."

"Yes," the Senator said brusquely.

"When you flew back east with your son's body, do you remember spending any time at the airport before taking off?"

"Not a minute!" came the quick reply. "Henry, my pilot, and the co-pilot were waiting for us when we drove straight to my plane with the hearse following, and they loaded the body in the rear compartment and we all boarded and took off immediately."

"Were Mr. Mason and Mr. Campion in the car with you?"

"Yes, of course. Why?"

"Just checking some details," I said, without sharing with the Senator that I had just discovered Campion in a straightforward lie.

"And you have nothing further to share with me?" the Senator asked, clearly annoyed.

"Not at this time, Senator," I said.

"Look, Lieutenant, I was told you were one of the best homicide detectives the city had. My son did **not...** I repeat, did *not* kill himself and I'm looking to you to prove that!"

"I'm doing my best, Senator," was all I could muster.

"If I have to hire a dozen private detectives, I will!" he said adamantly.

Now I was annoyed.

"That's always your option,' I said, "but you must see that there's very little to go on."

My challenge seemed to rein him in a bit.

"Yes, well, get back to me as soon as you have any new information," he said in a slightly calmer voice.

"I will, sir, and I'll see you tomorrow at the memorial service."

Senator Braxton expressed no surprise at my attending his son's service and said a hasty goodbye.

XIV

After a late lunch and a smoke on the way back to my office—I had succumbed to the temptation and bought another pack—I found a new fax from Tom Corrigan.

Hi George, As you requested, here's the phone log for the lodge. No surprises here, as far as I can see. Any progress? Tom

I eagerly studied the phone log. On the night of David Braxton's death, there were six calls made between 6:05 and 6:59 P.M.: One to Washington D.C. from 6:05 to 6:15—that would have been to Senator Braxton; one to New Haven, Connecticut from 6:16 to 6:33—Professor Jenkins; three to New York City—the first one from 6:35 to 6:41—the number was Campion's home; the second one from 6:44 to 6:50—Mason's home number; the last one from 6:51 to 6:57was, I felt sure, Campion's lawyer, whom he had mentioned calling. I thought briefly about questioning this lawyer but knew that he'd claim lawyer-client confidentiality so I dismissed that idea. The final call at 6:59 was to Tom Corrigan's office. Mason and Campion had been very busy on the phone almost from the moment that David Braxton died.

What caught my attention was the order of these calls. Professor Jenkins was the second person that Campion and Mason called, before they called their wives and before Campion called his lawyer. And they had spent the longest amount of time talking to Jenkins. Tom was wrong; this was a surprise.

Now I wanted to follow up on another detail. I flipped through my notebook and found my summary of my interview with Peter Campion. When I had asked him about the notes he had written on his idea for a documentary, he said he had gone over them at the airport while the plane was being refueled and then discarded them. He lied. Why?

Tom Corrigan's notes were in a file folder sitting on my desk and I started reading them again. I found the part where both Mason and Campion had heard the one shot and, first, Campion and, seconds later, Mason rushed out of their rooms, down the stairs and into the living room where they found Braxton's body. I recalled something that now seemed significant: the architectural detail of the three men's bedrooms having interior windows overlooking the two-story living room.

If you heard a shot coming directly from below, why wouldn't your natural instinct be to step to the window and look down to see what had happened, rather than rushing down the stairs as both men reported they had done? When I was a kid playing in the street in front of our apartment house in Brooklyn, if I, or any kid, shouted in distress, all the mothers would rush to the windows of the front rooms and not come running into the street. I had to speak to Peter Campion and confront him with these inconsistencies. But first I had more homework to do.

I had already asked Tommy Clancy, a detective a few months away from retirement who wasn't serving on any active case, to check the newspaper morgues of *The New York Times*, *The Daily News* and *The Post* for all clippings on the three men and David Braxton's family. Now I called the archives division of the public library, identified myself, and asked them to get everything they had on David Braxton, Peter Campion and Jack Mason ready for me to pick up later that afternoon. Mrs. Paterson, the lady who handled my request, identified herself as the archives supervisor.

"You're not giving us much time to gather so much information about three such prominent families," she grumbled.

"I realize that," I responded, "but I can't stress enough how important this information is to my current police investigation."

I paused, letting my last line sink in.

"Naturally, this is all very confidential," I added in a conspiratorial tone.

The three names I had just given her had been splashed all over the papers for days, and unless she had been in a coma, she'd couldn't help but make a connection.

"I really need your help." I pleaded, hoping she'd see herself and her crew as a vital backup to the long arm of the law.

"We'll do our best, Lieutenant," she said in a more upbeat tone..

"Thank you, Mrs. Paterson. I know I can count on you and your terrific staff," I said in a totally phony vein.

I felt I needed to be better informed before I observed the entire cast of characters assembled at the memorial service. I was doing more homework on this case than I ever did in college, and I hoped that it would pay off.

XV

At home that night surrounded by books and files of press clippings that I had picked up from Mrs. Paterson in the late afternoon, I was determined to learn more about the world that David Braxton inhabited and about the guy, himself. So I stocked up on cold beer and a fresh pack of cigarettes, forgetting to feel guilty, and read for several hours, skimming books, magazine articles and newspaper reports until I was too tired to read any more.

Among the many interesting things I learned from all this reading—it reminded me of my last-minute, late night cram sessions for college exams—was that The Hundred Club is just about the most exclusive private club in New York, if not the country. You can only be invited to join if you have distinguished yourself in some field other than entertainment—no actors, comics, jugglers or ventriloquists need apply, thank you very much, and even playwrights are frowned upon. From its start-up date in 1820, membership was limited to one hundred; hence, the name.

No one ever applied for membership; you had to be nominated by a minimum of three members and then your candidacy was reviewed by a committee of seven members, at which point any one of those seven members could blackball you. If the committee of seven passed you, you then needed a simple majority of the remaining ninety-three members, minus the three who had nominated you, at their annual meeting and you were home free. It seemed easier to get into heaven than to gain admittance to this group. I couldn't imagine jumping through all those hoops, but except for the PBA's bowling league when I was a young cop and eager to fit in, I'd never been a joiner

Membership in The Hundred Club was not passed down from one generation to the next and it wasn't until the nineteen-seventies that women were considered for admission. A Nobel Prize winning scientist, a Pulitzer Prize winning author, a Charles Lindberg or a Thomas Edison were viable candidate types—Lindberg and Edison had actually been members—and captains of industry were considered but only if they had been great benefactors to society. Some Rockefellers made it on this basis, as had David Braxton, the youngest member ever to be elected. Peter Campion and Jack Mason were not members.

The Braxton pharmaceutical fortune, currently estimated in excess of three billion dollars, had been started by William Braxton, David's grandfather, and inherited by Senator Lawrence Braxton and his two younger siblings, Harriet and Henry. It seems Henry had become the typical playboy, marrying a succession of Hollywood actresses and café society ladies, only to be killed in a car crash when he was barely fifty, leaving no heirs. Harriet was a reclusive poet, living on a vast estate outside of Litchfield, Connecticut, where she grew orchids, bred champion Irish Wolfhounds and wrote poetry, shunning the limelight and never marrying.

Before pursuing political office, Senator Braxton had managed the family-owned company, multiplying its assets many times over, but was not a philanthropist. Grandpa William Braxton was still alive when David was born and was so delighted to see his line continuing through male heirs that he established a multi-million dollar trust fund that David inherited on his twenty-first birthday and immediately put to good use by using half of his millions to establish the Braxton Foundation.

This foundation underwrote such worthy local causes as refuge houses for battered women, seed money for start-up community organizations, free tutoring programs in low-ranked school districts and the preservation and restoration of historically significant New York buildings.

As I read through the newspaper files, reporting on both David Braxton's personal exploits and his philanthropic work, I was genuinely impressed. This guy really knew how to live. He had gone on archeological digs in Asia and Africa, was an avid mountain climber, had sailed around the world with his two buddies, Mason and Campion, before any of them were married, joined a scientific expedition in the Amazon that he underwrote, served on the governing boards of two museums, the Philharmonic Orchestra, the Public Library and a ballet company. He played the harpsichord, was a competitive bridge player and collected rare manuscripts and French Impressionist art. He was a regular participant , along with Mason and Campion, in the New York Marathon, and all three repeatedly finished in the top fifty.

And then there were the five foreign languages he spoke—fluently, I now learned, and Nadira had forgotten to mention Italian—and the two others he could read. I had to laugh when I remembered how at Queens College I had to take a brush-up course in English grammar. Of course I could recite Latin, thanks to my memorizing all the responses to the Mass as an altar boy, but I didn't have the slightest idea what most of it meant. Latin in high school meant memorizing verb declensions—amo, amas, amat—and stumbling through Caesar's Gallic Wars—All Gaul is divided into three parts. I could also claim to be fluent in three dialects: Brooklyn, Bronx and Queens-Italian.

While a lot of young guys were burning their draft cards and running away as far as they could from the Vietnam War, Braxton, at twenty-one, straight out of Yale, volunteered to serve, and he demonstrated great bravery in Nam as an officer. Mason and Campion had followed his example and also enlisted.

Braxton was a licensed pilot and flew his own plane. He had volunteered several times to fly in supplies at his own expense to areas of our country devastated by some natural disaster. He was an ardent supporter of wildlife and donated loads of money to animal rights and preservation organizations, as well as supporting local dog and cat shelters.

Toss in all the photos of the beautiful women he dated— when did he find the time?—until, at thirty-four, he married Nadira, the greatest beauty of them all, and you had a bird's-eye view of a fabled life right out of some romantic novel. He had crammed so much living into his forty-four years that his New York Times obituary sounded like that of a man who had lived well into advanced age. But the fabled life ended suddenly, tragically and mysteriously, and it bothered the hell out of me somehow that a guy who had little in common with me except that we both inhabited the same planet, had fought in Nam and lived in the same city, had had his good fortune reversed and died so early. This wasn't just a challenge to my professional reputation; I had to find the answer for my own sense of justice, my own peace of mind.

I slept fitfully that night, dreaming of climbing snow-drenched mountains and hanging precariously over dizzying precipices.

XVI

The Hundred Club, for all its exclusivity and illustrious membership, was not what I had pictured. Although the portraits of most of the founding members looked down with austere expressions from the dark green walls of the Main Lounge where the memorial service was to take place, the furnishings were old and shabby. Then I reflected that these people didn't have to impress anyone. The more current members were to be seen much less grandly in photographs lining the marble staircase that led to the Main Lounge on the second floor of an old five-story limestone building, darkened with age and sitting defiantly between two gleaming steel skyscrapers in the middle of Manhattan.

At one end of the cavernous lounge was a battered looking podium, surrounded by tasteful floral arrangements, including orchids that I thought may have come from the Connecticut greenhouse of Harriet Braxton, the Senator's spinster sister. I congratulated myself on making this connection thanks to all the reading I had done last night on the Braxton brood.

I could imagine the noted personages who had stood at that podium, and today would be no exception . Small folding chairs had been arranged in rows facing the podium, with large wing-back chairs, that I assumed were pieces of the room's usual furniture, placed in the rear. Two large fireplaces were situated about twenty-five feet apart on the inner wall and the opposite wall's windows were covered in heavy velvet drapes, wine colored and visibly dusty. The lighting, low and subdued, came from wall sconces that lent sinister shadows to the portraits lining the walls.

I had no trouble getting into the club, having given my name to the man seated at a desk just inside the heavy oak entrance door. He directed me to the staircase to the side of a vestibule lined with Quaker style benches, on which a few elderly patrician types were seated. I climbed the stairs and stationed myself, inconspicuously I hoped, just to the side of the wide entrance to the lounge so I could observe the participants' arrivals without being noticed.

The service was scheduled for 2 P.M. and starting at 1:30 a small number of mourners trickled in, mostly rail-thin elderly ladies in smart looking dark suits with tight, dyed hair recently coifed—my first wife loved the word coiffure, along with cuisine and hauteur, and always tried to include them in any conversation she was having with anyone she was trying to impress. Now I guessed she could get her *coiffure* done every day and eat nothing but rich *cuisine* and speak with *hauteur* to everyone she met. What a phony! Anyway, the frail old ladies walked gingerly to the large wing chairs, sitting with sighs of relief.

By 1:50 I estimated the room was two-thirds full, with many faces and names that were known to the everyday public.

Then I saw a lady I guessed to be in her sixties, ramrod tall and cadaverously thin, dressed in severe, shapeless black, walk slowly down the center aisle, her head downcast, looking neither to the right or the left, and take a seat in the front row. This, I assumed, was Aunt Harriet, Senator Braxton's sister, the poet and semi-recluse.

Jack Mason and Peter Campion, accompanied by their sleek, elegant wives, arrived together at about 1:55 and made their way slowly toward the front rows of seats, their progress interrupted by whispered greetings and sympathetic pats on the shoulder from the one-hundred-fifty or so assembled guests. Campion looked drawn and tired; Mason looked like a man who was falling to pieces and would collapse at any moment.

I recognized many people from their pictures in the papers or on television or, in some instances, on magazine covers. The wealth and power concentrated in this room was staggering, I reflected. I counted seven United States Senators, eleven congressmen, a former ambassador to Great Britain, two former supermodels besides Nadira—in my book they couldn't compare to her although they were beautiful—a woman who had occupied three high level positions during two administrations but whose name I couldn't recall, several CEOs of major American or international companies, a Nobel Prize winning author and many men and women celebrated for their philanthropy and love of the arts. Family names known for generations to the public were well represented. I also spotted three noted television personalities besides Peter Campion.

I couldn't help but notice the restrained manners of all these celebrated people, so different from any service I had attended for, say, one of my Italian relatives or friends. Here I saw low-voiced greetings and firm handshakes between the men and air kisses between the ladies: everything hushed, subdued and formally proper. No bear hugs and real kissing; no little cries of joy at distant relatives' seeing each other for the first time after many years, and no displays of grief, whether real or pretended, to add to the drama of the occasion. You see, in my crowd, wakes and funerals were seen as theater, in which everyone played a role. The rules of conduct for this crowd were polite but distant and ultimately, I thought, prescribed and cold.

Precisely at 2 P.M. Senator and Mrs. Lawrence Braxton entered the room and while they smiled warmly at the assembled people, they did not pause for any individual greetings but proceeded up the main aisle and took the first two seats to the left of the podium. Immediately after they were seated, Nadira came into view, surrounded by her children. She paused for just a second at the entrance, surveying the scene, and again I was nearly hypnotized by her extraordinary beauty and regal bearing. She was dressed simply in a dark gray suit with black high heel shoes, and her hair was swept up into a complicated twist at the back of her head that accentuated her long neck and flawless complexion. Her large dark eyes swept across me for a moment with no hint of recognition and I saw her diaphragm expand with a large intake of breath before taking the hands of her two youngest children, the five-year-old twin boys, and with the oldest child, a girl, following closely behind her mother, Nadira marched up the aisle, looking straight ahead and settled into the remaining seats in the front row, opposite her in-laws.

In the brief time span I had observed her three children since arriving at the top of the stairs, I was struck by how different they were from my kids at their ages. No matter what the occasion we attended with them—funerals, weddings, baptisms, graduations or any church service, we could never get them to sit still or shut up until they were practically in their teens. But today, on this solemn occasion, the nine-year-old girl and her two younger brothers had a quiet look of gravity that wasn't only the naturally sad appearance of young children reacting to the death of their father. Rather, it seemed to be an inbred recognition of the suitable air of solemnity that this occasion warranted.

I thought of all the newsreel pictures I had seen of Carolyn and John-John Kennedy during their father's funeral and how the three Braxton children, sitting quietly now in their seats, not fidgeting, looking straight ahead, reminded me of them. With my kids at that age, I thought, if the entire family was wiped out—mother, father, aunts, uncles and the two remaining grandparents—as devastating as that would be to them, they still couldn't sit still for more than thirty seconds and could never have attended any service without insisting on carrying a doll or stuffed animal for the two girls and a soldier or truck for my son. Within five minutes after the service had started, they would have been wondering aimlessly about the room, staring at the people they didn't know, and shortly after that, inventing some game that involved running or hiding, accompanied by a lot of giggling and taunting. If I scolded them, their mother would have reproached me with her magazine-learned lingo about crushing their spirits or not letting them give vent to their natural instincts. I smiled to myself, remembering scenes in restaurants and museums and movie houses, and our endless debates on what was appropriate behavior, and all my ex-wife's accusations about my rigid, militaristic approach to discipline.

Then I thought about how all three of my kids had changed after we got divorced. It was like they took a giant leap forward and were eager to please us while they were with each of us—their mother commented on this remarkable change too. Even my son, who resented Ginny for replacing his mother as my wife, tried to keep on good terms with me. The counselor I had been seeing after my divorce suggested this was because they didn't feel they were on as firm a footing as before and were afraid they might lose one or both of us if they didn't shape up. Whatever their motivation, they went from being the typically whinny suburban kids to being cooperative, compassionate and just damn pleasant company. And now, with Emily, nineteen, in college and George Jr., sixteen, a junior in high school, and sweet Beth , thirteen, just starting high school, I was really proud of the way they were turning out. They were sane, goal-driven kids, despite all the things their mega-bucks stepfather could throw at them

My thoughts were interrupted by some club employee turning on and testing the microphone system, followed shortly by Senator Braxton's rising from his seat and going to the podium. There were not enough seats for everyone and I moved forward and took a position against the wall among a group of men, and from here I had a clear view of all the people in the first rows. The Senator's strong, deep voice soon filled the room but it was less assured, more tentative, occasionally rising in pitch and then descending to a whisper, as he clearly struggled to maintain his composure. He welcomed everyone and then spoke for only a few minutes. His concluding comments were quite moving.

"My son, David, was an extraordinary man who led an extraordinary life and leaves an extraordinary legacy. He lives vividly in the hearts of his mother and myself, his brother, Thomas, and his two sisters, Margaret and Elizabeth; in the all-encompassing love he shared with his wife, Nadira, and his three children, Alfred, Kenneth and Eleanor, and in the loving memories of his many friends, and the countless good works his Foundation has done. From the age of thirteen he adopted a view of life that was remarkable for one so young and that can best be summed up in one of his favorite quotations: 'The great business of life is to be, to do, and then depart, knowing you have sucked the very marrow of life fearlessly in the constant face of death.' However short his destiny, he fulfilled his dreams and we are all the richer for having had him in our lives. May his endlessly zestful, loving spirit find everlasting peace and may 'trumpets bring thee to thy rest.'"

I was listening to Senator Braxton but I was watching the other mourners in the first row, particularly Campion and Mason. Neither man was looking at Senator Braxton. Campion was staring straight ahead as if in a trance, and Mason, tears streaming down his cheeks, was clearly struggling to keep his composure. He was leaning into his wife who held his hand and kept whispering in his ear.

Thomas Braxton, David's younger brother, now rose to speak, and I mentally reviewed the information I had gathered on David's siblings. The two girls, Margaret and Elizabeth, were closer in age to David—forty-two and thirty-nine respectively— while Thomas was a full eleven years younger than his brother, probably an unexpected surprise. It wasn't just an eleven-year age gap that distinguished Thomas from David; the two men could not possibly have been less like each other.

The girls resembled their older brother and father, so much so that they might be called handsome women but they would never be described as pretty. Like David, they had both graduated from Yale but not at the top of their class. Margaret had gone on to Yale Law School and become a civil rights lawyer, then married Lewis Thornton, a self-made millionaire and, like his brother-in-law, a noted young philanthropist. Elizabeth had gotten a master's degree in social work from Columbia University and headed the

Braxton foundation that David had started when he came into his grandfather's trust fund. As yet, she had not married.

It was interesting to note, as a matter of public record, that not all four Braxton children had been treated the same by Grandpa Braxton, David's trust fund was significantly larger than his sisters' and Grandpa was dead by the time Thomas came along.

Thomas Braxton was vastly different from his older, idolized brother and two sisters. He took after his mother and was small and slight and much fairer than his handsome, strapping siblings, with a shy manner and a gentle personality. He, too, had attended Yale but had dropped out in his sophomore year, due to some mysterious illness that had been widely rumored in the papers to be a nervous disorder. He had taken up painting—as therapy? I wondered—but had held no exhibitions in the ensuing years and now, at thirty-three, had not married and lived with his Aunt Harriet at her Connecticut estate and was as reclusive as she.

I watched him as he adjusted the microphone on the podium—he was a good five inches shorter than his father—and gave a nervous half-smile in his parents' direction. I saw his mother bow her head and return his smile, as if sending him waves of encouragement. He clutched the podium with both hands and began to speak in a low, halting voice, keeping his eyes down and never looking at the audience.

"John Milton wrote: 'That which before us lies in daily life is the prime wisdom.' My brother David was, next to my parents, the most important influence in my life. Because of our age difference, he was really more like a second father to me rather than just an older brother. I knew at an early age that he was a person of exceptional gifts and talents, many of which I could never hope to equal. Yet he was so loving, so sensitive and understanding that he always urged me to be my own person and to live, not in the shadow of his own accomplishments, but in the fullness of my own capabilities and personal pursuits. Above all, he encouraged me to emulate him in only one aspect: to live life to the fullest—every day, every minute, every second. He had such a deep appreciation for the gift of life that it is hard, if not impossible, to accept the contradiction of his having renounced it. He was..."

Thomas's voice faltered at this point and he stared at the podium, seemingly lost in the confusion of his thoughts, tears flowing down his cheeks. As though embarrassed by this display of raw emotion, the audience, like one organism, waited silently, hardly breathing, hoping for Thomas to regain his composure, but he could not.

"I'm sorry," he stammered, his voice cracking. "Please forgive me." He turned toward his parents, his face now a contorted mask of anguish, and rushed back to his seat between his mother and his Aunt Harriet and bowed his head as both ladies tried to comfort him. Senator Braxton looked flushed, whether from sympathy or embarrassment for his son, I couldn't tell.

Peter Campion rose and moved quickly to the podium, removing notes from the inside pocket of his dark blue suit and placing them before him. In his best professional manner, honed by so many hours delivering news and discussing current events in front of television cameras, he began speaking, and his clear, soothing voice filled the room, relieving the awkward tension felt by Thomas's hasty retreat.

"David Braxton radiated life like the sun radiates warmth. An outsize personality whose engine was a huge heart, he was a fountain, a geyser, a volcano of joy and zest and bravery and warmth that was contagious to all who came within his orbit. From the first day I met him when we were both thirteen and David and Jack Mason and I were assigned as roommates in our first year of prep school, until the last day when this extraordinary light was untimely dimmed, he was my friend, my confidante, my companion, my booster, my inspiration. 'To whom much is given, much is expected.' David was blessed with so much but unlike many men who take everything for granted—physical gifts, superior intellect, an advantageous position in society—David was always mindful, ever conscious of his blessings and keenly felt the responsibility to use his talents and advantages not only to savor every second of his life but to be a magnet for others to fully appreciate the gift of life."

"Then why the hell did he take his own life?" I shouted to myself in frustration as Campion continued.

"Among boys, and later, men, he was a natural leader, possessing an abundance of sterling qualities: courage, audacity, loyalty, compassion, empathy, generosity and a loving heart. He was both an idealist and a pragmatist who faced life with brutal honesty, knowing its fleeting, unpredictable nature; lessons underscored by his wartime experience as an army officer in Vietnam, about which we seldom talked, but for which he received an array of medals, including the purple heart. His sharp and ready wit and his self-deprecating humor made him the best companion. He was the most generous of friends, giving his time and support and encouragement as well as a ready ear and an open mind. I remember when my son was born prematurely and I was in Bangkok on assignment..."

Campion now told a series of personal stories involving him and David or him and David and Jack Mason, all with the point of illustrating the many fine qualities of the deceased. I listened with half an ear and growing frustration. Was I the only person in the room who saw the irony of all this talk about David Braxton's great zest for life and the generally accepted notion of his having blown his brains out for no apparent reason? My frustration was deeper than that, I had to admit. Every word, every sentence that was spoken here today seemed to contradict the apparent suicide of this guy who, even I had come to see, was special—a cut above us ordinary mortals.

It simply didn't make any sense. I knew it and I felt it in my gut and I was getting madder and more frustrated each day. His father and his wife didn't believe it either, but his two closest friends said that was what happened and because of their long, close friendship with the deceased, that became the accepted story.

Now I reviewed the tiny cracks in their story. Like Campion's lie about reading notes at the airport while the Senator's plane was being made ready for the return flight to New York. And all the seemingly inconsequential questions surrounding the suicide scene: the half-empty whisky glasses; the description of rushing downstairs after the shot was heard instead of looking out the interior windows of their bedrooms that looked directly out on the living room below; even the location where Braxton shot himself, never moving from the sofa where the three friends had just ended having a few drinks and some laughs. There was another answer to this and I had to find it. What were Campion and Mason hiding?

Campion came to the end of his memories by quoting Emerson: "A friend may well be reckoned the masterpiece of nature." He followed that up with a quote from Robert Browning: "Life, struck sharp on death / Makes awful lightning," and ended with one final quote from Euripides: "Who knows but life be that which men call death / And death what men call life."

Being with this crowd was like getting a college education all over again, I thought.

Campion calmly returned his notes to his jacket pocket and walked to his seat. There was a brief, awkward interlude as no one came to the podium and guests looked around in confusion, thinking perhaps that the service had ended. Then I saw Mason's wife whisper something to him and as though coming out of a trance he rose and walked stiffly like a robot to the podium, clutching a sheet of paper in his hand. For what seemed like a long time he stood silently at the podium, staring down at the sheet of paper he had placed on the podium's shelf and when he finally began to speak, it was in a low monotone.

He started reading a poem, "To An Athlete Dying Young," by A. E. Housman. His voice cracked and he paused, staring fixedly down at his paper until he could continue.

When he finished the poem, for the first time he looked up and across his audience, staring at the opposite wall.

"This should never have happened," was all he said and I remembered so clearly that these were the same words he said to Tom Corrigan the night of David Braxton's death.

The Unitarian minister thanked everyone for coming and concluded with a brief prayer about the immortality of the soul being the legacy left by the human spirit.

Nadira and her children stood up and moved to the entrance of the Main Lounge where she stationed herself to greet the guests as they solemnly filed out. I took up an inconspicuous spot across from her and was fascinated to see the poise and composure and graciousness with which she thanked each person for coming and frequently added a personal note such as "David was so fond of you," or "You were always a loyal friend to David."

Only when Campion and Mason embraced her did I notice a stiffness or hesitancy in her response, but that was understandable, given their evidence about David's suicide which she did not, could not accept.

Suddenly a tall figure in black was at my side and half turning I recognized David's Aunt Harriet.

"I understand you're the detective my brother has asked to look into David's death," she said in a near-whisper so no one could overhear.

"Yes, ma'am," I answered.

"I'd like to see you in private. Could you spare me a few minutes?" she asked, not imperiously as I would have expected someone of her wealth and age to speak, but imploringly, as if she were begging me for a great favor.

"Of course," I said.

"Good. My car is just outside. I'll wait for you."

"No need to wait," I said. "We can leave now."

She gave me a shy smile and I followed her down the marble staircase and out the front door where a line of limousines was waiting. Hers was the third one in line and a uniformed chauffeur opened the door. I followed her into the limo and quickly saw that David's brother, Thomas, was sitting on the side seat, looking totally distraught. Then I remembered that Thomas lived with Aunt Harriet.

"I'm sorry, I don't know your name," Harriet said and again I was struck by the gentleness of her manner.

"Detective Lieutenant Russo," I said.

She gave me a small smile and shifted her eyes from me to Thomas. Like many shy people, she found it hard to maintain eye contact for very long.

"Lieutenant Russo," she began, still staring at Thomas, "I know my brother has told you of our doubts regarding the circumstances of David's death. Knowing David as we all did, we just can't reconcile the way he lived his life with the taking of it."

"I can't either," I said, shaking my head in agreement.

Another small smile.

"Last night Thomas recalled something that David had said to him when Thomas was only about nine or ten. David was home from Yale for Christmas. Thomas remembered it because in some ways it was so out of character for his adored older brother to say. David was always so jolly and upbeat."

I shifted my gaze to Thomas whose eyes were red from crying, and he was still struggling with the sniffles. Thomas blew his nose again and then spoke in that same low, hesitant voice I had heard at the memorial service, but this time he gazed off in the distance and he seemed to be reliving the scene he was describing.

"It was Christmas morning and we had all opened our presents—father and mother and Aunt Harriet and Elizabeth and Margaret and David and myself. David had given me a pair of hockey skates and a copy of Thoreau's *Walden*. 'It's never too early to start reading Thoreau,' he said as I unwrapped the book. 'I was reading him at about your age and he had a tremendous influence on my life. Sometime, when you're older, I'll tell you about it.' After breakfast we were all going down to the pond to skate, and David came to my room to see if I was ready, and I thanked him for my skates again. 'The skates you'll probably grow out of by next winter' he said, 'but I hope you grow into Thoreau.' I laughed but was curious about anything my big brother was interested in, so I asked him, 'Has Thoreau really influenced you that much, David?' and he replied, 'Thoreau and others.' Then he looked off through my window down to the pond and his voice changed and he said, 'I try to live every day as if it were my last, because one day it might be.'"

Thomas paused and I could see more tears coming and I jumped into the silence.

"Your recall of that exchange is quite extraordinary for one so young when it took place, and considering that it was so many years ago," I said, instinctively playing detective because one word Thomas had quoted his brother as saying sounded an alarm in my brain.

"That's because Thomas has kept a diary since he was about eight," Aunt Harriet said, smiling at Thomas and patting his knee. "He was always interested in writing and I had given him one on a previous Christmas, and last night he read his diary entry describing that exchange to me."

"And you're sure he said 'might' and not 'will'?" I asked Thomas.

Thomas looked momentarily puzzled, blinked a few times and then reached down and pulled a leather briefcase from beneath his seat. Opening the main compartment, he pulled out a small leather-bound notebook with faded gold lettering that I could still make out as "Diary of Thomas Murchinson Braxton." He turned to a page already bookmarked and briefly read its contents before nodding yes and handing the diary to me. Sure enough, it was worded exactly as Thomas reported. Still, I wanted further confirmation.

"You're positive these were your brother's exact words?" I asked.

Thomas thought for a moment before answering.

"Yes, I'm sure they were, because I was so struck by them that after he left my room and before I joined everybody at the pond, I wrote in my diary what David had said to me."

Now I was thinking out loud. "If he said 'will,' that would reflect the certainty of death that every human will face, but saying 'might' suggests a conditional or unforeseen circumstance that could result in death. I might get hit by a bus if I don't watch when I'm crossing a busy New York street, or I might get cancer if I don't stop smoking—actually, I've told myself that many times and still continue to smoke, playing against the odds that I can beat the deadly results of my habit. David's use of 'might' suggests the attitude that death could occur at any time and not as some inevitable end to a normal life span."

Aunt Harriet was quick to respond. "But that fits perfectly with David's lifestyle! Whether he was climbing mountains or exploring jungles or fighting the Vietcong, he was always taking chances, living life on the edge. He seemed to relish it."

My mind darted back to the note David Braxton had written to his wife when their first child was born; the note Nadira had shared with me. That, too, had curious wording, suggesting a preoccupation with death at the ripe old age of thirty-five—and now, with this recorded conversation, when he was no more than nineteen or twenty. My thoughts were interrupted by Harriet's sweet voice.

"Did you know that David wrote a novel?" she asked.

"No, I didn't," I answered, surprised.

"Oh, it was never published," she said quickly, "and he was very young. It was the summer of his senior year at Groton and he was spending part of the summer with me in Connecticut. I suppose the story was somewhat typical of an idealistic teenager, except for the advanced vocabulary and serious theme. He told me he did it as a lark and he dedicated it to me. I was very touched."

"Does it still exist?" I asked.

Harriet smiled. "Yes, it does." She reached for the briefcase from where Thomas had taken his diary and took out a large manila envelope. Handing it to me, she said, "I don't know if this is any help, but it certainly demonstrates, even as a teenager, how much David valued living life to the fullest."

I took the envelope and thanked her.

"I've enclosed an envelope with my Connecticut address," she said. "Please send it back to me when you've read it. I made you this copy but I don't want David's writings inadvertently made public so that's why I'm asking you to return the manuscript when you're finished.."

She paused, then gave me her shy half-smile.

"We all loved David very much and we're determined to find out what really happened. We're grateful for any light you can throw on this terrible tragedy, Lieutenant."

"Do you believe that Campion and Mason are lying?" I asked bluntly.

She looked startled and then sad, and when she finally spoke, her voice had a steeliness that I had not heard before.

"Everyone in the family loves Peter and Jack, and we know that they loved David and he, them. But they're hiding something, of that I'm sure."

I nodded and opened the door of the limo but Aunt Harriet grabbed my arm.

"Oh, one more thing, Lieutenant. I don't know how this could be of any help, but you might want to speak to Professor Jenkins, David's philosophy professor at Yale. All three boys seemed to be heavily influenced by him. David was always making some reference or other to him."

"I will," I said and closed the door, then watched the limo make its slow departure down the street.

XVII

I lit up a cigarette and sucked the smoke in greedily, feeling both ashamed and happy, then started walking. A half-block away from the One Hundred Club, I came upon Peter Campion hailing a cab. I stepped up beside him and took him unawares. I had instantly decided on a frontal attack strategy and started speaking loudly in his ear.

"Hi, Peter. Your little story about reading the notes for your supposed documentary was a pack of lies," I said quickly. "Both Senator Braxton and the airport manager contradict you.." I was lying about the airport manager but threw him in anyway. "The Senator wants to know why you claimed that his plane was delayed." Another lie.

Campion was standing between two parked cars, his arm extended in the New York gesture for hailing a taxi. He never looked directly at me but his facial expression changed from calm to alarmed. I had definitely caught him off-guard and now that I had his attention, I decided to follow up with a one-two punch, but this time I was bluffing.

"And your story about rushing out of your bedroom and down the stairs when you heard the gunshot is a lie, too, and I can prove it."

I watched Campion's face turn red.

"So you better get those high-priced lawyers of yours lined up, my friend, 'cause you've got a lot of explaining to do."

Campion never turned to look directly at me. A taxi pulled up and he rushed forward to open the door and threw himself in, clearly wanting to get away from me.

"Be seeing you!" I shouted in as threatening a tone as I could muster before the door closed and the cab pulled away.

I felt good about this little scene and hoped it would put him off balance. He was such a smug bastard, beneath his veneer of suave geniality that I kept fighting the urge to take a poke at him. At least I had now gotten some verbal shots fired off.

XVIII

Checking in at my office I found another message from Tom Corrigan.

Hi George, Here's an interesting tidbit for the big-city detective. I met Mrs. Jenkowski coming out of church on Sunday and we were chatting a bit and the topic got around to David Braxton's suicide. She mentioned that every year on the last night of their visit, she was asked to prepare a dinner for the three men in advance and then told to take the night off. I had thought it was only this year that she wasn't present at the lodge during the last night of the men's vacation, but evidently this was the standard practice. For what it's worth, just thought I'd pass it along. Any new slant? Regards, Tom

Sadly, I had to admit that there wasn't any clear new slant—just a lot of loose ends, contradictions, suspicions and endless speculations. This new revelation only added more questions to my growing list. Why did they insist on being alone every year on the last night of their stay? Was it for some harmless guy talk—dirty jokes and bragging about sexual exploits or reliving their war adventures in Nam—without the presence of any woman? Or was there something more sinister? And if it was just for fun and male bonding, why would Braxton choose that time to kill himself?

I asked myself, what's wrong with this scene? One minute Braxton is relaxing with a few drinks, laughing and joking and having a good time with his buddies. He even offers to heat up the dinner that Mrs. Jenkowski prepared while his two friends retreat to their rooms for a while. The next minute, without any warning, he's blowing his brains out. Ridiculous, I told myself.

I recalled the other piece of information that Tom had related to me, about Mrs. Jenkowski saying that the men's mood always seemed to sour as the end of their stay drew near. Why? What the hell were they up to? Frustrated and cranky, I stuffed the message in my pocket and headed for home, prepared to spend the evening reading David Braxton's adolescent manuscript to see if that could shed any glimmer of light on all this confusion.

XIX

After a quick dinner of Stouffer's Microwave Lasagna, two beers and a tossed salad, I was just getting settled in my leather recliner with Braxton's manuscript and a brand new pack of cigarettes that I had guiltily bought on the way home, when the phone rang. I picked it up and heard the sweet voice of my daughter, Emily.

"Hi, daddy." she said, and I could instantly see her pretty face, which seemed to always be smiling—she was that continuously cheerful a kid!

"Hi, Em," I said, involuntarily breaking out with my own smile. "What's up?"

"Nothing much," she replied with a slight giggle. "I just came back to the dorm from the library—I've been studying for a Spanish test—and I was feeling a bit down so I decided to call you. I'm glad you were home."

One thing I knew for sure: If Emily was feeling a bit down, it wasn't because of anxiety about any test, since she was a straight A student, not like her old man.

"What's got you down?" I asked in my typical detective follow-up questioning mode.

"Oh, nothing in particular, I guess...just some things in general...I worry about you, Daddy."

"Now why should you be worrying about me?" I asked, taking a long drag on my cigarette.

"Daddy, are you still smoking? " she asked in a louder tone. "You promised me you were giving it up." Her voice was filled with hurt and worry. "You promised!" she said, and her accusation stung.

I knew she'd caught me so I decided not to lie but to slant the truth.

"Em,, honey, it's not as easy as you think. I am giving it up but it has to be gradual, so I'm cutting way down...just one or two each day, and then I can kick the habit for good."

"But you've been kicking the habit for a long time now!" she said, and while the accusatory tone was still evident, her voice was milder.

"Well, at least I'm still trying," I offered in my defense.

She came at me from a different angle.

"Are you eating proper meals?" she asked solicitously, and I realized that she had truly become my little mother.

"Yes," I answered brusquely.

"What did you have for dinner?"

Again I decided on an evasive action because the mere mention of any dish cooked in the microwave would verify to her that I'm living in a substandard way. I affected a cheerful, enthusiastic voice.

"I stopped at Rosselli's and brought home some delicious lasagna and a nice tossed salad," I said, referring to a restaurant not far from our house that she knew well.

There was a pause and then she said in a sly voice, "But, Daddy, Rosselli's doesn't have take-out."

"They make an exception for me," I lied. "Now let's change the subject. How's Georgie?"

"Georgie's having girl trouble," she said, heaving a sigh of an indulgent older sister. "Connie told him she didn't want to go steady but wanted to date other boys."

"Well, then he can play the field too," I said off the top of my head.

"But, Daddy, you know how shy Georgie is!" she said, and now she's being indulgent with me. "He doesn't want to play the field. He wants the security of dating one girl that he feels comfortable with."

"Then he'll just have to adjust," I said unsympathetically, and she heaved another sigh but changed the topic.

"I wish you weren't living alone. Are you seeing anyone?" she asked tentatively.

Now this first child of my loins, whom I loved more than life, itself, and who loved to play mother to me, and for the most part I found it cute and indulged her, had just stepped over the line, and I can feel my face turning red and my discomfort level rising.

Almost by telepathy, she seemed to realize that she'd gone too far and she said, "I don't mean to pry. I just want you to be happy, Daddy."

She makes this statement in a voice that's filled with such genuine concern and sweetness that my indignation immediately receded as a wave of affection rushed over me.

"Don't worry so much about me, Em. I'm doing fine," I assured her, but her little interrogation had forced me to acknowledge, only to myself, that I wasn't in such great shape as I pretended to be.

I searched for another topic since my children and I had a pact that we never talked about their mother or their life with their stepfather, but, being kids, things always slipped out. I knew that he was good to them. As a matter of fact, he was spoiling them with expensive vacations and expensive toys and expensive clothes. I knew I could never compete with him and I consoled myself with the attitude that he was trying to buy their love but I was still their dad and, I hoped, solid in their affection. Emily's solicitude for me, although challenging at times, seemed to prove my theory.

"What's Beth up to?" I asked, eager to change the subject and knowing that Emily loved her sister and acted like a mother to her, too.

Her voice took on a lighter shade and her words came faster.

"Beth tried out for the junior cheerleader squad and she made it!" she said with genuine excitement.

"That's great!" I said, trying to match her enthusiasm. "We'll have to celebrate."

"Are we seeing you next weekend?" she asked, her voice again taking on a tentative tone, as though she was never sure when she could count on seeing me. And I had to admit that there had been times, because of work, when I had disappointed all three of my kids after making plans to do something special together.

"Absolutely," I assured her. "I'll pick you up at six on Friday."

"No, Daddy. I'll drive Georgie and Beth to you. The car finally came."

Now I remembered that Tony, my ex-wife's current husband, had given Emily a car for her nineteenth birthday several weeks ago, but it had been on back-order because of the special color combination she wanted. My mood turned sour for a moment as I recalled that I had given Emily a boogie board that she raved over, but any fool knows that a brand new car beats a boogie board any day. There's nothing like a stepfather giving your kids expensive gifts that you can't afford to make you feel like shit. I swallowed that sour feeling.

"Okay, but drive carefully," I urged. "Remember what Matt told you about the statistics on teenage fatalities resulting from speeding." I was referring to a good buddy of mine from the

Academy who was an instructor for the Emergency Vehicle Operation class and knew my kids well.

"I will," she said good-naturedly. "We'll see you around six."

I knew what was coming next, for she always ended all her phone calls to me with the same sentence and no matter how many times she said it, my heart always swelled in my chest.

"I love you, Daddy."

"I love you, Em."

I hung up and reminded myself that when I took the kids out to dinner that weekend, not to go to Rosselli's.

XX

I reached for another cigarette, feeling more guilty than usual after telling my daughter that I was cutting back, and picked up the Braxton manuscript. The phone rang again. Annoyed, I picked it up and grunted "Hello."

"Is this George Russo?" asked a woman's voice that was vaguely familiar but I couldn't place it right off.

"Yes," I answered in a milder tone because the voice was intriguing.

"Well, this is someone from your past," the voice said teasingly, and then it clicked.

"Theresa!" I shouted, actually rising from my chair in my excitement and surprise, spilling the manuscript on the floor.

"None other," she said, waves of laughter rippling across her voice, opening memory vaults that had been locked for many years. "Do you forgive me for calling you?" she asked, still in a light vein.

"Hell, yes," I said, still shouting in my enthusiasm. "I'm really happy to hear from you. John O'Shea told me you were back living with your parents. I was going to call you."

"John told me he had seen you and mentioned you were going to call me. But since this is the age of equality and I'm an ardent feminist now, I thought I'd call you and see if you've evolved enough to be okay with me making the first move."

"I hope I passed the test," I said honestly, as old images of this vibrant, beautiful girl flooded my brain.

"So far, so good," she said, still with that teasing tone.

"How are you?" I asked, really wanting to know, and suddenly hoping to reestablish old intimacies.

"I'm fine," she said and there was a pause. "No, wait a minute. I'm not fine, but I'm okay. At least I'm well on my way to a full recovery after breaking up a relationship that lasted almost eight years."

"I heard about that from John," was all I could think of to say by way of offering any consolation.

"Yeah, my batting average isn't very good, George. At least you and I parted as friends who just drifted apart," she said, and I found myself shaking my head in agreement, struck by her honesty. "I can't say the same for my husband and now Steve, my ex-partner. Lots of bad feelings there."

"I'm sorry," was all I could muster.

"They just didn't consider infidelity any big deal," she said, a darker tone slipping into her voice. "And I do."

Not knowing how to respond to this statement, I just said, "Yeah."

"Anyway," she continued on a lighter note, "I'm back with my parents living in my old room but not for long!"

"Oh?" I said, feeling that my conversational skills were back to the junior high level.

"I managed to get a degree in accounting from Puget Sound University while I was married, and I just landed a job in Manhattan and I've put a deposit on a condo in Forest Hills," she said in one long breath, which made me smile.

"Congratulations."

"What's up with you?" she asked, and before I could answer, she said, "I heard about you losing your wife to cancer. I'm so sorry, George."

"Yeah, that was a shock," I admitted, "but life goes on," I said, letting her know in a not-very-subtle way that I was now ready for a new relationship.

"And how are your kids? You have three, right?"

"My kids are great. I was just on the phone with my oldest daughter, Emily, just before you called."

"I tried calling before and the line was busy, so I figured you were involved with a hot new romance," she said, clearly teasing.

"No hot new romance just yet. I've been waiting for you," I said, returning her teasing tone.

"You mean we should take up just where we left off about twenty-eight years ago?" she continued teasing, "Under the boardwalk."

"That's not a bad idea," I shot back, appreciating her acknowledgment of the special bond we shared in losing our virginity to each other.

Her voice changed and took on a deeper tone.

"I'm a little shell-shocked just now with everything that's happened in the love department but, honestly, George, I do need a friend."

"I am your friend; we've just been separated for a long time," I said.

"What a nice thing to say!" But you were always a pretty nice fella."

"Look, Theresa, I'm on a big case just now and I have a lot of homework to do tonight, but I'd love to see you and catch up. Why don't we get together for dinner some night soon?"

"I'd like that," she said.

We decided on a date.

"It's really great to hear from you," I said, and she said "I'm looking forward to seeing you," and then we hung up and my brain was still buzzing with happy thoughts of her, but I had to get down to business with Braxton's manuscript.

XXI

The manuscript was titled *Deathly Blessings,* and I was back in my leather lounge chair, starting to read it. Now I've never been much of a reader, especially of anything that could be considered good literature. The only reading of this kind that I ever did, besides *Moby Dick* and *Huckleberry Finn* and *The Scarlet Letter* in high school, for which the Cliff Notes came in handy, was my two required English courses at Queens College where I made an honest effort but ultimately resorted again to published shortcuts to see me through the final exams. So I'm about thirty pages into Braxton's manuscript and my eyes are already glazing over and I'm struggling to focus.

I don't know if this is any good but I do recognize instantly just from the vocabulary, long, winding sentences, the lengthy descriptions of people and places and the plot intricacies that at seventeen, Braxton's mind was light years ahead of mine. At that age I was only interested in meeting girls, making out, rock and roll, and keeping my beat-up old Dodge shining.

With grim resolution I forced myself to continue into the heart of the story about a celebrated philosophy professor at an anonymous university who learns when he is fifty-seven that he has an incurable cancer and is given less than a year to live. At this point the professor examines his life and realizes that he hadn't lived it according to the philosophy that he had personally embraced, *carpe diem* or "live for the day." Lots of characters surround this professor—family, colleagues and students—and Braxton included lots of philosophic discussions which was really heavy going for me and I skipped over a lot.

The professor decides that in the few months before he's expected to become incapacitated, he'll live his life to the fullest. He retires, gives most of his possessions to his children and friends, which sure makes them happy but also gives the professor great satisfaction, and, with his wife, embarks on a European tour, visiting the libraries of famous universities and dining at the very best restaurants of every major city they visit.

In describing some of the meals that the professor and his wife enjoyed, Braxton lost me at the first wine that was served. Even the salads included ingredients I had never heard of. So after about six weeks of living high on the hog, the professor returns home and devotes nearly all his time to learning the harpsichord, thus happily fulfilling a long-cherished dream.

When he's finally laid low by the ravages of his cancer, his family marvels at his resignation and happy frame of mind. At his request, his wife and children take turns reading to him, but what does this philosophy professor request? Children's fairy tales.

When they're not reading him fairy tales, he's listening to his favorite Wagner operas. Here, again, Braxton takes you into the professor's mind as he interprets and responds to the singers and the musical motifs, the complicated plots and the multi-layered orchestrations. I waded through as much of this as I could, but my eyes closed and my head nodded three or four times before I admitted defeat and skipped to the last section.

The professor realizes that, except for the last few months, he's wasted his life, studying and lecturing on the philosophies of others, all the while not living for the intense joys that daily living can bring if lived on a truly conscious path for self-fulfillment. As his capacities slip away, he decides to end his life and save his family the agony of witnessing a slow, painful death. He devises a clever way of doing this, without informing or involving his family.

I skipped over the details of how he secretly hoards pills and skimmed through the final death scene that, as Braxton described it, is strangely upbeat, with the professor's last word being "Joy!"

I checked my watch and realized that except for brief dozing-off periods, I had been reading for nearly four hours—a record for me. My mind was numb and I couldn't think about anything except bed. But as I was brushing my teeth on automatic pilot, one thought suddenly surfaced: I had to speak to Braxton's favorite philosophy professor, Professor Jenkins at Yale, the one that Campion and Mason had called the night of Braxton's supposed suicide. Even Harriet Braxton, David's aunt, had suggested that I speak to him. He clearly played an important role in the lives of these three men, and perhaps he could shed some light on David's death. It was worth a try.

XXII

Two days later I was on my way to New Haven. I had called Professor Jenkins at his Yale office on Wednesday morning, the day after reading Braxton's manuscript. I identified myself and asked if I could meet him to discuss David Braxton.

"I'd be happy to meet with you, Lieutenant," Jenkins replied, but in a tone that seemed full of sad resignation. "I have only one class on Thursday morning that ends at eleven. Meet me at the Philosophy Department office and you can follow me home. My wife will make us some lunch."

This was my first visit to Yale University. I arrived in New Haven quite early and I decided to park my car a good distance away and walk across campus to the Philosophy Department, stopping at the library and the athletic building. The only Ivy League school I'd ever seen before was Columbia University in the early 1970's, when I was a young cop and we were called to control the riots that were breaking out on campus in protest of the Vietnam War. After my own experience in Nam, I was now secretly in favor of these protests but never expressed my opinion because of the strong bias on the part of most of my fellow officers against the protesters—cops who, I should add, had never been to Nam. Columbia's concrete campus, smack in the middle of an old, deteriorating and dangerous section of upper Manhattan—I'm happy to report that it got better in the late 1980's—was nothing like Yale.

As I strolled among the Gothic buildings, some actually covered with ivy, and visited the hushed atmosphere of the library with its dark timbered ceilings, large fireplaces and austere portraits, I have to admit that I was awed by the tradition and exclusivity that this school represented. This was a far cry from Queens College, I told myself. I could see many members of The Hundred Club fitting in here perfectly and I thought about the informal classes of society that separated someone like me from a David Braxton or a Jack Mason, starting at birth.

I had never even dreamed of going to an Ivy League college. I wasn't even sure I could make it in any four-year college and I had little to guide me. My father was a garbage man for the New York City Sanitation Department, and my mother was a housewife who spoke more Italian than English. In the tough Italian neighborhood of Bensonhurst where I grew up until I was fourteen and my parents moved to Queens, the aspirations passed down to my generation were to get a job right after high school, say, with the fire or police or sanitation departments—some civil service job that offered security, health benefits and a pension. Then you got married, had your family and eventually bought a house in the suburbs but not so far away that you couldn't trek in most Sundays for dinner with the folks. Case closed; life over at forty!

I had pretty much followed that master plan: joined the police force when I got back from Nam and a few years later got married at twenty-five—most of my buddies had married at younger ages but I had to wait an extra couple of years for Carolyn to make up her mind between me and Mr. Up-And-Coming. My parents didn't approve of my marrying Carolyn because she wasn't Italian and she came from Yonkers, and right from the start they said she put on airs. They were right.

Just about the only thing we did differently from the other couples we knew was to space our kids out a little bit—they were all three years apart—because Carolyn suffered from intense post-partum depression and after that passed, she was always worried about getting her figure back. After Georgie was born, she was adamant about not having any more kids, and Beth was an accident after an engagement party for some cousin of hers when we both had had too much to drink. The only time I even thought of hitting her was when she said something about an abortion but she saw my reaction and I guess she was more afraid of me than of having another kid.

Once I was on the police force, I easily adjusted to its semi-military pattern, with the street cops taking orders from the brass, and with even the same titles as the military—sergeant, lieutenant, captain. But something inside of me said, you should try to climb the ladder and be one of the brass. So, with little confidence, I took my credits from Queensborough Community College and enrolled at Queens College, having moved to the Elmont section of Queens at Carolyn's insistence for what she convinced me would be a better life for our family. It wasn't.

I took night courses for the next three and a half years to earn my bachelor's degree. During all that time I recognized that I was just going through the motions and getting the barest amount of any real education out of my college experience. It was just a means to an end. I was a practical man with a practical goal; not some idealistic kid with his head in the clouds. I needed this degree, this piece of paper, to make my way in the world. Sometimes, though, I would sort of daydream how nice it might be to be a full-time student without any other responsibilities except to listen to lectures and read and write and think. The hushed atmosphere of the Yale Library made me recall that daydream.

I left the library and strolled along winding tree-lined pathways, looking at the faces of the students passing me in the opposite direction: white, Asian and a few black. They all seemed to me to have an earnestness, even an indefinable air of superiority, secretly knowing that they were the lucky ones who had made it to one of the peaks of the academic world and already had their ticket to success and riches. I wasn't jealous of them; I simply marveled at their good fortune in inhabiting a different sphere.

I pictured David Braxton and Peter Campion and Jack Mason in this environment, at ease, taking it for granted, so natural in their leadership roles, effortlessly excelling academically while also participating fully in campus life, including, I recalled, three varsity letters, the debating team and several clubs. It must be genetic, I concluded, as I reached the impressive building housing the Philosophy Department, checked my watch and realized I was ten minutes late. I quickly mounted the steps leading to the front entrance of what was to me an alien world.

XXIII

"Lieutenant Russo?" I heard my name as I approached the entrance and turned to see a stout, disheveled looking man in his sixties, at least five inches shorted than my six feet, with a wreath of white hair whirling about his head with each gust of wind, a jowly face, florid complexion and the merriest eyes I had ever seen except for Christmas cards with Santa Claus on them. As a matter of face, if you put a beard on him, he would have been the spitting image of the vision of Santa Claus that I had as a kid.

"Professor Jenkins?" I asked, walking toward him, my hand outstretched. "Sorry I'm a little late."

"Not a problem," Jenkins said, flashing me a megawatt smile that scrunched up his whole face and accentuated chubby dimples. At that moment he *was* Santa Claus and I wanted to tell him what I wanted for next Christmas. His furry white eyebrows seemed to have a life of their own, moving continuously up and down over his warm, blue eyes. I liked him immediately. I could also imagine why David Braxton liked him, besides any intellectual bond, when I compared this happy, rumpled little man with the grave, commanding presence of David's father, the august Senator.

"Follow me," he said cheerfully and was off at a surprisingly rapid pace for a man of his age and stoutness.

"I parked on the other side of the campus and walked across," I quickly explained.

"I'll drive you to your car and then it's only about fifteen minutes to my house," he said.

When we reached my car, he double parked and waited for me to pull out behind him before driving away. Professor Jenkins drove like he walked: fast!

The speed limit was forty-five but my speedometer read fifty-nine as we quickly passed through several New Haven neighborhoods and headed for a suburb. Finally we slowed down in front of an old Victorian cottage, set far back from the quiet tree-lined street. We both pulled into the driveway that led to a detached garage in the rear of the house, but Professor Jenkins stopped in front of the house and I pulled up behind him. He got out of his car and we walked briskly across a gravel pathway leading to the front door.

"Now for some of my wife's delicious homemade pea soup and a walnut salad and a fresh loaf of her homemade bread!" Jenkins said, rubbing his hands together in gleeful anticipation, like a child on Christmas morning. His enthusiasm was contagious.

We reached the door, which wasn't locked, and immediately entered a cozy, low-ceiling living room with an old-style fireplace and bookshelves on either side, crammed with books in disarray. A large wooden coat rack stood next to the front door on which Jenkins hung his coat and mine, while calling out, "Hildi, we're here!"

The living room flowed into the dining room and off to the side of that must have been the kitchen. A very tall, thin, stately looking woman with white hair and black eyebrows appeared and came forward to greet us. She spoke with a distinct Scandinavian accent. She was polite but a little reserved and definitely not the Mrs. Claus type I had been half expecting.

"Hildi is chairperson of the Anthropology Department," Jenkins said with obvious pride, and I assumed he meant at Yale.

Hildi said nothing, just smiled and led us into the dining room where a large salad bowl, a bread basket, filled water glasses and table settings for three were already in place. Hildi motioned me to a chair and then produced from the kitchen a large covered soup tureen and placed it in the middle of the table.

"A specialty of the house!" Jenkins exclaimed as he removed the lid and steam rose into the air. He motioned for me to hand him my bowl and filled it with soup.

"I forgot the croutons," Hildi said, rising quickly and moving into the kitchen and then returning with a bowl filled with croutons.

"They're homemade too," Jenkins informed me with a wide laugh. Santa Claus clearly enjoyed his domestic life.

There was something so attractive, so enticing about this jolly, energetic man that I could just picture him in front of a large classroom filled with Yale students, selling them on the beauty and wisdom and importance of philosophy. No wonder David Braxton loved him, I thought, this time with envy, as I flashed back to the gallery of tired, mostly uninspiring teachers I had experienced in my night classes. Of course, I had never taken a philosophy course. I knew a few philosophers' names—Aristotle, Plato, Socrates, Voltaire—but never thought about what they had preached or how they had viewed life. I guess I was too busy scrounging around and struggling to meet the demands of my own life to sit back and ask myself what it was all about. But when Ginny died, that was the only time I asked myself what the hell was the purpose or plan of all this. It seemed so unfair, so arbitrary, so random. Then I got mad and then I got drunk for a pretty long time and then I stopped thinking about anything. When I sobered up, I stopped feeling sorry for myself and got on with my life, immersing myself in my work and in trying to be a good father to my kids.

Now here was this man, Jenkins, who had devoted himself to philosophy but he didn't seem different from most other guys, only, somehow, happier. I wanted to ask him some questions about his area but was afraid of sounding stupid. Instead, he was asking me lots of questions about police work all during lunch, with Hildi beaming at us and saying little..

After our soup and salad and delicious bread, Hildi brought out a big platter of homemade cookies and served us coffee. Jenkins reached eagerly for the cookies.

"Be sure to sample everything," he said. "There's chocolate chip and oatmeal raisin and molasses. I never can decide which one I like the best. Oh, and sugar cookies, too!"

Hildi laughed and filled a plate with a sample of each kind of cookie and handed it to me. She was definitely warming up as she saw the way I devoured her meal.

"They really are good!" I said, as crumbs escaped down my chin and I returned Hildi's beaming smile

When I finished the cookies on my plate, both Jenkins and Hildi insisted I take some more and I eagerly accepted their offer while picturing my paunch getting a little bigger. I'm not your stereotypical donut-eating cop, but I can compete with anyone on the force when it comes to pizza. Anyway, these cookies really were special, and Jenkins, too, was taking a second helping. Hildi had none but clearly enjoyed watching us consume her offerings with such gusto.

"Why don't we have our coffee in the den," Jenkins suggested, then smiled sheepishly. "That way, I can smoke a cigar, which is the only room in the house where I'm allowed to smoke."

"And when you're finished with the nasty thing," Hildi said in what was clearly a teasing tone as she touched her husband's arm, "be sure to use the can of Lysol spray I left by the door of your den so you don't stink up the rest of the house."

"Yes, Mrs. Jenkins," Jenkins said good humouredly, rising from the table with his coffee cup in hand.

"Thanks for the great lunch," I said, as, with quick strides, Hildi carried dishes into the kitchen.

"Sorry it couldn't be more," Hildi said over her shoulder, "but I have a class in half an hour and then a department meeting."

I could picture this strong, vibrant woman giving a commanding lecture to eager undergraduates and then chairing a meeting of her peers with efficiency and authority, all in a day's work. I hadn't taken any anthropology courses in college either, so I was way out of my league in this household, but they had made me feel both welcomed and comfortable. What a team they made! I was feeling so relaxed that I almost forget my mission in coming to New Haven. Now, alone with the professor, I would get the information I had come for.

XXIV

I followed Jenkins toward the back of the house and into a small room, also filled helter-skelter with books. There was a roll-top desk and two leather arm chairs with small side tables. Jenkins settled himself into one and motioned me toward the other. On the table next to his chair was a small humidor from which he took a cigar and rolled it between his fingers.

"It's my one vice," he said, smiling. "Well, this and a good martini; sometimes too many. Would you care for one?"

"A cigar or a martini?" I quipped, knowing what he meant.

Jenkins gave a belly laugh that resonated around the little room and made me think that I had just said something hilarious.

He extended his hand holding a cigar but I shook my head. "Never acquired the habit," I said, "but I'll join you with a cigarette."

"Never acquired the habit," Jenkins said quickly while nodding his permission, and I resolved to finally quit smoking as soon as this pack was finished. Then I thought about the half-filled carton at home and changed my resolution to when that was empty.

"I didn't ask you if you minded cigar smoke," Jenkins said, holding the cigar in one hand and a lighter in the other.

"Not at all," I said quickly. "Been in too many all-night poker games to mind. Besides, my father used to occasionally smoke a cigar when I was a kid and he would let me cut the tip for him, which always made me feel important."

We both smiled, and Jenkins extended his lighter to my cigarette before lighting his cigar. We smoked in silence for a few moments as I gazed around the room, noting several pictures of children.

"Are those your children?" I asked, pointing to the pictures.

"We have no children," Jenkins said, exhaling a cloud of cigar smoke with obvious pleasure. "Those are my nieces and nephews." He said nothing more on the subject and I didn't press him.

Then I spotted a picture of David Braxton, Peter Campion and Jack Mason, all young and smiling, with their arms around one another's shoulders. Jenkins followed my gaze.

"Yes, that's the famous three amigos," he said, and his voice took on a deeper register as he, too, gazed at the picture. "The three most brilliant students I ever had! We all became very close. They were like family to me."

"I understand that Campion and Mason called you on the night that David died, shortly after they discovered his body."

The smiling, wistful look on Jenkins' face changed noticeably, and I could see that he was now on alert. He took a long puff on his cigar and flicked the ash off the tip into an ashtray on the table next to his chair. Then he put the cigar down on the side of the ashtray and looked directly at me.

"Yes," was all he said in a somber voice, and the feeling in the room had changed dramatically.

"Would you mind sharing with me what they said to you in that phone conversation?" I said, locking eyes with him.

He visibly flinched and gazed off into a corner of the room, and I saw tears in his eyes. When he finally spoke, his voice had a low, far-away tone as if he were talking to himself, reliving the moments of that phone call.

"It was so unexpected, so shocking! They were broken up, crying like little boys, especially Jack. Peter was on the phone and eventually got control of himself, but Jack was standing at his side and I could hear his sobs. I was speechless, could barely breathe, much less talk."

I broke into this mental reverie with, "But what did they say?"

Jenkins' gaze shifted back to me. He picked up his cigar and inhaled, letting the smoke out slowly before answering me. Tears were now visible at the corners of his eyes.

"I'm afraid that's personal and private," he said with finality.

"Wait a minute," I said, leaning forward, my voice rising in pitch. "A brilliant young man, with everything to live for, gives no warning and suddenly kills himself. The two men closest to him, and present in other rooms when he does it, call you within minutes of his death, and you say that whatever they said to you is personal and private?"

Jenkins' face had slumped into a determined scowl. "I'm afraid so, yes."

I was getting heated now.

"You realize, Professor, that no one in David's family believes he killed himself, despite what Campion and Mason are saying. Furthermore, I've weighed all the evidence and uncovered some contradictory clues that lead me to feel certain that he didn't kill himself."

I was exaggerating here to see how Jenkins would respond. He was clearly uncomfortable.

"If this matter were brought to court, you could be forced to testify as to what the two men said to you or be charged with obstructing justice."

I watched Jenkins' face collapse in confusion and I felt sorry for the guy, but why wouldn't he tell me what the hell was said?

Still not looking directly at me, Jenkins put his cigar down again on the ashtray, folded his hands and placed them on his lap.

"They were just very, very upset," he finally said. "And because we had all been so close, I guess they wanted me to console them."

Jenkins was growing more upset and his voice quivered, "But I couldn't. I couldn't believe..." His voice trailed off.

All my accumulated experience as a detective, as well as my gut feeling, told me he wasn't telling me everything. I couldn't press the guy any further or he'd collapse completely, so I took a different tack.

"You didn't attend David's memorial service. Why?"

"I wasn't invited," was his straightforward answer, but I could sense the hurt behind the crisp response.

"Why not?" I asked.

He ran his left hand through his unruly white hair.

"There was no reason why David's wife would invite me. I only met her once at their wedding. David preferred to keep his relationship with me separate from his family. So did Peter and Jack."

"You said that the three of them were the most brilliant students you ever had?"

Jenkins seemed to barely hear me but finally nodded, yes.

"Professor, I don't know anything about philosophy, so help me out here. What would a philosophy major study?"

My question seemed to break the downward slide of Jenkins' pitiful mood. He swallowed hard and wiped his stained cheeks with a quick swipe of his hands."

"You start with a course in Logic, along with learning philosophical terminology and definitions as a basic starting point for discussion. You then take several survey courses covering the great thinkers of the Pre-Christian era, who influenced the culture, religion and outlook of Western Civilization. Then you examine the thinkers of the Christian era and their contributions to shifting perspectives about life and man's place in the universe. Finally, if you declare your major to be philosophy at the end of these survey courses, and if you are accepted by the department, you take advanced, in-depth courses on the philosophy of individual thinkers. Then, as a senior, you select some philosophic question—like What is Beauty?—that's approved by your advisor and write an exegesis on that topic, demonstrating your grasp of preceding philosophic strands in defending your own hypothesis about the comparative merits or imperfections of a particular school of thinking."

Jenkins rattled all this off like he was saying the Pledge of Allegiance, as my mind struggled to keep up. What the hell was an "exegesis"?

"You were David's advisor, I take it?"

"I was advisor to both David and Peter and knew Jack very well," Jenkins replied, a smile returning to his face as he picked up his cigar again. "They were very special."

"In what way?" I asked.

After several puffs on his cigar, Jenkins returned it to the ashtray and looked off to the corner of the room.

"Yale is filled with very bright students, of course, but I found over my many years of teaching that a good number of them are what I might call 'academically gifted.' That is to say, they have been good students all their lives. They study, they pick things up quickly, they learn, they can express themselves clearly in verbal and written modes, and they regurgitate back to their teachers those things they feel their teachers want to hear."

Jenkins waved his hand to clear away some of the smoke from his cigar.

"Mind you, there's nothing wrong with that. They've got the academic system down pat, from kindergarten to graduate school, and they go on to distinguish themselves in many fields after their education has ended, applying the same set of skills to different circumstances and bolstered in their confidence by having been validated by the leading universities as gifted and talented."

Jenkins paused and I wondered where this monologue was leading, although I had to admit it was interesting, especially the part of being validated as gifted and talented. I guess to a large extent we see ourselves as we think the world sees us. That's why I wanted to be Detective Lieutenant Russo instead of just plain Officer Russo—for a little more respect.

Jenkins now looked directly at me and smiled.

"But my goal is not to teach **about** philosophy, which is okay for the undergraduates just sampling a few philosophy survey courses, but to show some special students how to think like a philosopher. And if you think like a philosopher, that has to affect how you live, because philosophy is all about the principles and beliefs by which we live. To *live* a philosophy, one must be able to examine oneself objectively and compare how one is living against the set of principles one's private philosophy embraces. In other words, philosophy is really not theory but rather putting theory into action, as we go about our daily lives. We take in the world and test our responses to it, and our actions in it, against our set of beliefs and observations. As a philosopher I believe in a life well lived, so you should be able to see in my actions and attitudes that I treasure life and try to extract the fullest measure of pleasure from every second of it."

Like any good teacher, Jenkins paused and seemed to be examining my facial expression for signs of understanding. I gave him a half-smile in return, for I thought I caught the gist of what he was saying, although I honestly wasn't sure. He took another puff on his cigar and continued.

"David and Peter and Jack were among those rare students who saw the central role of philosophy as a guide to everyday life and had the ability to be 'in the moment,' as I like to say, to step outside of themselves and always be thinking about their actions and consciously evaluating them. All three of them *lived* their philosophy."

"What was David's topic for his final paper?" I asked.

"Typical David!" Jenkins said as a big smile creased his chubby cheeks. "He took an obscure German philosopher of the early nineteenth century and created an extravagant hypothesis and then defended it brilliantly. The entire department read it and everybody said it should receive highest honors. No, not everybody, now that I come to think of it. A few old professors who had spent a lifetime expounding a different philosophy of life and saw their views challenged by David's assertions, were quick to defend their positions against David's. They aggressively raised questions and objections with him, but David just smiled and then answered them with his characteristic lucidity.

The sheer logic of his argument, in abstract philosophic terms, was impossible to refute. The rest of us got a big chuckle out of that because David was probably forty or fifty years younger than his adjudicators, but his mind, his thinking, his clarity of vision, was on a higher level. We all recognized that. He was simply the most outstanding student any of us had ever come in contact with during all our teaching years."

"And what about Campion and Mason?" I asked.

Jenkins chuckled.

"They were both outstanding, too, but David was the leader, the alpha of that three-man pack. When you're dealing with truly brilliant minds, your own limitations make it difficult to render such finite distinctions, and perhaps it was David's extraordinary articulateness and great charm that caused me to see him just a tiny bit ahead of his friends. Jack didn't major in philosophy although he, too, was a philosopher in practice, as was Peter, certainly."

Then his face collapsed again. "It doesn't matter now," he said, looking away from me. "I'd hate to believe that I, in any way…" His voice trailed off and then he stopped in mid-sentence, looking embarrassed.

"What did Campion write about for his senior paper?"

Jenkins' reply was spontaneous.

"His paper was equally brilliant but much less controversial," he said, almost in a whisper.

"What was so controversial about David's paper?"

"Well," Jenkins said, and then paused as if weighing his words carefully, "It was the conclusion he came to, although at the time I never thought…"

"And what was that conclusion?" I asked, interrupting him, my curiosity fully aroused.

Jenkins sat motionless in his chair but I could tell from his eyes that his mind was fully engaged with what seemed like some battle that was taking place within him. Finally he stirred.

"Why don't you read it for yourself?" he said

"Where can I get a copy of David's paper?"

Jenkins hesitated for only a moment, as if pondering the questions, and then rose from his chair and headed toward his roll-top desk.

"Right here!" he said, pulling out a bottom drawer and, after rummaging through its contents, withdrawing a faded blue folder.

"You kept a copy?" I asked, clearly surprised.

"Yes," he said, walking toward me and extending the folder. "Why wouldn't I? David was like a son to me. I just never thought…" Again he abruptly stopped speaking and slumped back down into his chair, his hands covering his face, his head bent.

I rose with the manuscript under my arm, patted Jenkins on the shoulder, quietly said "Thank you, Professor. I'll see myself out," and left.

XXV

David Braxton's senior philosophy paper was one-hundred-thirty typed pages, plus another thirty-five pages of end notes and a lengthy bibliography. The longest paper I had written in college was a straightforward history of the F.B.I that was fifteen typed pages with the widest margins I could get away with.

Back home that night, after reading the first twenty pages of Braxton's paper, I realized that, once again, I was way over my head. The vocabulary, technical terms, marathon sentences—by the time I got to the end of one of these, I had forgotten everything from the first half—complex philosophic histories and intricate explanations made me feel like I was reading something in a foreign language.

My first thought was how shortchanged I had been in my own college education in comparison to this level of writing, analyzing, setting up a proposition and defending it in blazingly beautiful prose and intricately woven arguments. My second thought, more self-serving than the first, was that I was trying to understand one of the most brilliant minds that Yale's Philosophy Department—no, since he graduated number one in his class, possibly the entire Yale faculty—had ever encountered. I chuckled to myself when I thought of my mother's bragging about how smart I was when I got stars on my drawing of letters in first grade—an auspicious beginning to an academic career that quickly petered out when I hit long division and parts of speech. Yet I was determined to make some sense of this man's thinking.

I struggled on, late into the night, constantly referring to the dictionary at my side. How could one man know so many words I had never heard or seen before? I took notes, often going back to reread paragraphs until I could distill one simple thought that I quickly wrote down, even though it might be a total misinterpretation of what Braxton was saying.

After more concentrated effort than I had ever put into my own college studies, I decided that Braxton was tracing the line of philosophers who urged a *carpe diem* approach, or living life to the fullest in the present. He wove different strands of thinking on this subject into a complex pattern, citing many philosophers as different as Epicurus, Voltaire and William James—Voltaire being the only one I vaguely recognized—but focused primarily on a Max Luhrs, a little know German philosopher even in philosophic circles, who published a paper in 1821 called "Life In Death" in which Luhrs stated that one's life could only be truly appreciated and consciously experienced on a daily basis if one fully accepted, and lived with, the inevitable unpredictability of death.

I kept thinking of a picture that Sister Emmanuel, my sixth-grade teacher, had shown the class, which really grossed us out. It showed some monks in a monastery who adorned their doorways with all the skulls of the monks who had died in the previous centuries. But, according to Sister Emmanuel, the purpose for this practice was to remind the monks—and us—how fleeting and insignificant this life was, and the only thing that really mattered was getting to heaven in the next life. After seeing that picture, which she tacked up on the bulletin board in the front of the room, the only thing that mattered to us kids was getting the hell out of Sister Emmanuel's classroom.

As befuddled as I was by most of what I was reading, I was certain that this was not the approach that Max Luhrs was taking.

Max Luhrs claimed that man's challenge was to accept death as the persistent stimulus to embracing this life more fully. Death, as the correlative of life—- Braxton's phrase, not Luhrs and certainly not mine—must be acknowledged, accepted and confronted if life is to be experienced at the ultimate level of exploratory consciousness.

Braxton elaborated on that concept by offering some modern-day examples: The soldier in war—I could certainly relate to that; the bullfighter facing the charging bull; the circus aerialist performing sixty feet above the ground without a net; the fireman entering a blazing building to save a trapped occupant; the bungee jumper about to throw himself off a high bridge or cliff, the bungee cord his only connection to life; the test pilot on the first run of a new supersonic jet; astronauts strapped into their pod, sitting on the launching pad waiting for the rockets to ignite and hurl them into space—at these times Death draws near, sits on their shoulder and says, "Maybe...maybe not." When the outcome turns out to be "Not," how much deeper is their exhilaration not just in escaping death but in continuing to enjoy life.

The evening hours were passing quickly. I was smoking much more than I ordinarily did, lighting one cigarette with the stub of the previous one, and I had both eye strain and a headache.

I started thinking about Braxton's focus on living consciously in the present and thought about my own life: going through the motions of everyday existence, following the routines, meeting expectations, reacting to people and events—all without actively thinking about what I was doing or why I was doing it. I lived a lot in the future, thinking ahead to what I was going to have for dinner or what I'd do with my kids on their next visit or where I might go on my next vacation or endlessly fantasizing about women I would meet. Then I asked myself how often was I consciously aware of the current moment and what I was doing, and I had to admit it was very seldom.

Even my police work was done mostly on automatic pilot with only a few occasions calling for a sharp, in-the-moment focus. I flashed back to the time when I was a rookie cop walking a beat and had come upon a bank robbery in progress, spotting the hooded gunman through the front window of the bank, pointing a gun at a teller as she scooped money into a pillow case. A moment before seeing this scene I had probably been thinking about where

I'd eat lunch, but in an instant I was fully in the present and all my thoughts were focused on my next moves as my training took over.

I called for backup and then took a position in a doorway next to the bank. My entire body was on alert as I waited for the robber to exit the bank, mindful of all the passing pedestrians. Fortunately, my backup arrived and we caught the robber off-guard as he exited the bank and disarmed him without incident. I guess that at that point my mind floated away from the present and back to the future as I headed for lunch, but I could still remember how my senses seemed to be enhanced for the rest of the day.

I was certainly focused on the present, second by second, when I had gone to interview Nadira in her loft and took in every detail of how she looked, how she spoke, how she walked, how she smoked, how she smiled or cried, and any momentary physical contact I had with her. When I lit her cigarette and her hand touched mine—I could still feel that—as if all my senses had been heightened by her mere presence. But that was like when you have a dream and you're conscious of so many strange details that you ordinarily wouldn't be if it were real life. Being alone with Nadira was like being in a fantasy world and it didn't matter what circumstances brought us together: I was still living out a fantasy and enjoying every second of it.

Perhaps the one time I seemed to be fully aware of the present for any extended period of time was after Ginny was diagnosed and we knew there was a short time left to us and we packed every day with meaningful little things, enjoyed together:

walks, restaurants, movies, parties, outings with friends, picnics at the beach even in chilly weather. I remembered acutely how everything then took on an added dimension, an extra luster, as though we were doing these things for the first time and, like little kids, discovering the fullest pleasure and joy in our shared but limited time together.

At night, after our lovemaking, I would hold her tightly, knowing that she would be leaving me soon and mindful of how precious our remaining time together was. Even in sleep we'd cling to each other as if by physical force alone we could somehow postpone what we both knew was coming but never mentioned.

During her last days in hospice, sinking into unconsciousness, I held her hand and talked to her, not knowing if she could hear me but it didn't matter. I was living totally in the present, treasuring every minute that she was still with me. Then she slipped away, and with her went my consciousness of the present. Now I was either looking ahead, planning her funeral, thinking with dread of the empty years ahead, or looking back and reliving our happy life together. When I was in the present, I wasn't thinking at all but drinking heavily to blot out the pain.

Through the fog of those memories something new suddenly emerged: the realization that it had taken Ginny's death sentence to bring us the happiest, most prized, most fully enjoyed months, weeks and days of our married life.

Recognizing that all these thoughts were of the past and that my challenge in the present was to force myself to plough ahead with this interminable damn paper, I lit what was probably my twenty-fifth cigarette of the night and tried to focus. Sometime after 2 a.m., which was the last time I had checked my watch, I came to the last page. By now my mind was mush and I longed for sleep.

I gazed down at the notes filling the pages scattered before me and caught one paragraph that I had copied exactly from Braxton's paper.

"Man's challenge is to accept death as an intimate companion in order to embrace life more fully. Mindfulness— being completely, consciously in the moment—as the fullest quotidian capacity of sentient human beings, is a state that can only be achieved when one is also fully conscious of death, not as some vague, far-off abstract event, but as an ever-present possibility. To fully embrace this possibility is the surest way to achieve mindfulness and to enrich one's conscious pleasure in the inestimable gift of life."

Why did Professor Jenkins say that David Braxton's conclusion was so controversial? From everything I could understand, and that was damn little, I admit, Braxton was saying that the only way to live fully in the present moment was to bring death close to you in some tangible way. He had inserted a quote from Thoreau, "My life is like a stroll upon the beach, as near the ocean's edge as I can go." But then, in the margin of this page I saw how Professor Jenkins had scribbled another quote from

Thoreau: "It is characteristic of wisdom not to do desperate things."

Recalling all of Braxton's celebrated exploits, he certainly seemed addicted to living life on the edge: his volunteering for the Vietnam war and distinguishing himself as an officer; his daredevil physical pursuits like mountain climbing, free-fall sky diving and sailing solo great distances; his expeditions into the remote Amazon basin and Antarctica. Then why, I asked myself, would he take his life when the goal was to use the challenge of the imminent danger of death as a motivation to live life more fully? Then I saw one line from Braxton 's paper that caught my eye. It was a short quote from Elizabeth Barrett Browning: "Life is perfected by death."

I reread this line several times as brain waves rushed together and, despite my strained, over-tired condition, I had a flash of clear reasoning. This was the essence of what Professor Jenkins was referring to when he cited Braxton's "controversial conclusion." Now I thought I had the key to unlock the mystery of what happened that night at the lodge when David Braxton's life abruptly ended. I had the key to the puzzle but I was still missing some of the pieces.

XXVI

I slept late the next morning and woke up feeling like I had a hangover. I made coffee, showered and shaved and was happy to discover that I had one last pack of cigarettes left in the carton. I swore that after this pack I would quit, but as I lit the first cigarette of the day I was really savoring the action of inhaling the warm smoke, sucking it deep into my lungs and slowly letting it out through my nose. I smiled to myself, remembering David Braxton's writings on living fully in the present moment, as I was doing now, but then I thought of all the thousands of cigarettes that I had smoked out of habit, with no thought about what I was doing.

Braxton was right: we seldom live our lives in a fully conscious state. Had he achieved what seemed like a phenomenal leap? I reminded myself that he was an extraordinary person but then I also thought about the price he seemed to have paid for this achievement. Then my mind was drifting into the future as I planned my next step to unravel this mystery.

I called Senator Braxton at his office in the Senate Building and got his very pleasant secretary. She said he was chairing a committee meeting and wasn't expected back in his office until noon. I told her it was important for me to speak with him, and she promised to have him call me—I gave her my home number—as soon as he returned.

My watch said 10:55. I had another cup of coffee and another cigarette as I went over all my notes and made sure that every detail was committed to memory for instant recall as I envisioned the scene I hoped would soon take place.

True to her word, shortly after noontime, the Senator's secretary called me and then put the Senator on the line. I didn't waste time with pleasantries but cut right to the chase.

"Senator, I feel I'm very close to solving the puzzle of your son's death, but I need your help."

"What can I do?" was his straightforward response.

"Peter Campion and Jack Mason won't speak to me," I said, "but if you asked them to meet with you, I'm sure they'd come."

"I'm sure they would," the Senator said in a totally confident tone, and I had this fleeting glimpse of what it was like to march through life with such authority that just about everyone did your bidding. "Where would you like to meet?"

"It has to be some place private, and I'd like Nadira to join us," I said.

There was a pause and then the Senator said: "Nadira has taken the children to be with their grandmother at my home in Connecticut. She's leaving them there for a few weeks. Her apartment would be available."

"What about servants?" I asked, although I hadn't seen any when I had visited the apartment.

"The nanny is with the children and the cook is on vacation."

"Good," I replied. "How soon do you think you could set up the meeting?"

"I'll have to get back to you on that," the Senator said.

"I know you all live very busy lives," I said, somewhat stupidly.

"I'll try to get back to you this evening. Can I reach you at this number?"

"Yes, it's my home number."

"Very good," he said and I heard a click on the other end.

I spent a few hours at my office and then on my way home stopped at a drug store and bought a patch to help me stop smoking. I counted the remaining cigarettes in my last pack: I had ten left. I must have smoked eight cigarettes in the course of my afternoon, all automatically. I had to kick this habit. I stopped in at the local bar for a few beers and chatted with a few of the regulars and smoked a few more. I left the bar and picked up a take-out dinner at the Chinese restaurant next door. It was 6:30 when I got to my house and, by habit, flicked on the television to watch the evening news while I ate my sweet and sour chicken dinner with dumplings and fried rice. I finished off two beers with dinner and had a cigarette with my coffee and then had another one while watching *Jeopardy*.

I don't know why I watch *Jeopardy*; it only makes me feel stupid because I can come up with so few questions in most of the categories, except for sports or current events, or sometimes, politics. For all the other categories I sit there with no clue, while one of the three contestants gives an answer—in the form of a question, of course—before I can even wrap my mind around the clue. I wondered how a brainy guy like David Braxton would do on *Jeopardy*. Probably be the all-time champion.

Jeopardy was just finishing and, as usual, I couldn't come up with the question to Final Jeopardy when the phone rang and I heard Senator Braxton's voice.

"Lieutenant, everything is set for this coming Sunday, 8 P.M. at David's apartment."

"It must be just the five of us," I said automatically.

"Just the five of us," the Senator repeated, then added, "I hope you know what you're doing."

I wanted to sound more confident than I really was. "I believe we'll find the answer to your son's death, Senator," I said, still hedging my bet by carefully choosing to say "believe" rather than "know."

"I hope so," he said, and I could hear the anguish in his voice.

We said goodbye.

Sunday was four days away. I had set the scene; the players would be assembled. Now all I had to do was act on a hunch and a few scattered facts and hope I could meet the challenge of piercing the defenses of two brilliant, arrogant men. I was flying by the seat of my pants and I knew it. I reached for another cigarette, not bothering to count how many were left. I flipped through the pages of my notes for the hundredth time and saw that I had one more bit of research to do: the all-seeing eye of Buddha that the three men had taken as a central symbol of their lives when they were just teenagers. This case was taking me into areas of exploration that I never would have guessed I'd be venturing into, and it was both daunting and exhilarating.

XXVII

The next three days passed quickly because they were filled with good things that allowed me to get my mind off the Braxton case for a little while. That's not totally true since, no matter how hard I tried to follow Braxton's philosophy and stay "in the moment," my mind kept jumping forward to Sunday night and all the different ways my meeting with Campion, Mason, Nadira and Senator Braxton could go. I invented scene after scene, with the principal characters acting in different ways, and planned my reactions to their actions. Still, I knew in my gut that this was all a crap shoot and I tried my damnedest not to let my preoccupation with this coming event interfere with the personal pleasures at hand.

On Thursday evening I had my date with Theresa Costello. I picked her up at her parents house, and as I drove down Elm Street in my old neighborhood, memories came flooding over me. I suddenly felt like a kid on my first date and my heart was thumping in my chest as I parked in front of her parents' house. The funny thing is, Theresa told me later that she felt the same way and stayed up in her room doing extra primping while I made small talk with her parents.

I had always liked Mr. and Mrs. Costello, and they had always been very nice to me, back in high school when Theresa and I were going steady. It was shocking to me how much they had changed since I had last seen them but then I reminded myself how much time had passed. Mr. Costello offered me a drink, which I declined, and Mrs. Costello brought out a tray of cookies and I took one to be polite.

Small talk seemed difficult for them so I kept up the conversation by asking about families from the old neighborhood. We only chatted for about ten minutes, sitting in their small living room, or parlor as my mother called it, cramped with too much furniture that had been handed down from previous generations. I was looking back on my teens and thinking how nearly all the living rooms in these row houses in this section of Queens looked pretty much the same, with heavy dark furniture, frayed old carpets and lots of ornate lamps and bric-a-brac and pictures of relatives , both living and dead.

I heard Theresa coming down the stairs and then she was standing in the doorway. My heart did a little war dance as nearly three decades disappeared and I was back in high school, picking her up for the prom. She came toward me with that big, warm smile and I stood up and opened my arms and she unselfconsciously glided into them while her parents beamed.

She looked terrific. Her red hair was shorter but still framed her pretty features alluringly. Yes, of course there were a few lines around the eyes and mouth, but, if anything, she looked even prettier now than she did back in high school. As I returned her hug, I felt the wonderful curves of her fragrant body. She was more voluptuous than ever and old stirrings instantly came alive.

After a long embrace that had us rocking back and forth, we finally broke apart.

"You look great!" I said with total admiration.

"And you do too," she said, her voice full of excitement. "You haven't lost your hair, I'm glad to see, and I forgot how tall you were."

"I'm only an even six feet but you're just the right size to make me look taller when we're standing together. You always made me look good."

That wonderful twinkle in her eyes was there, just as I remembered it.

"And you haven't gotten fat!" she said, "but you're not the skinny kid any more either."

I involuntarily ran my hand down the front of my navy blue blazer, conscious of the small paunch I'd developed over the last several years, and sucked in my gut. I vowed right then to join a gym.

"I run two or three times a week when I can," I said, not elaborating on the inconsistency of my running schedule.

We exchanged other small complimentary remarks before saying goodbye to Theresa's parents and driving to my part of Queens for dinner at Rosselli's Restaurant.

I guess there's something special about adults who have shared memories of their formative years. Throughout the half-hour drive to the restaurant and then throughout dinner, what amazed me was the ease with which we picked up where we had left off so long ago. There was no awkwardness, no sudden bouts of shyness, no silences. We talked freely, sharing more of our recent histories, joking, teasing and flirting. I felt totally relaxed and happy for the first time since before Ginny got her diagnosis and it was great to be with a woman again and feel this good.

Theresa encouraged me to talk about Ginny, and I think I unloaded more of my feelings to her than to anyone else.. In turn, I was an attentive listener as Theresa spoke about the breakup of her long relationship, but where I was full of sadness over Ginny's loss, she was sad from being hurt over her boyfriend's betrayal. Without stating it, it seemed clear that we were both at a crossroad in our lives, trying to put the past behind us but not sure how to approach the future. But what I remembered most about the evening was the high spirits and laughter and being caught up in her warm personality, sparkling eyes and pretty face.

The hours slipped by unnoticed and after our second espresso and a shared tiramisu that Theresa ordered and insisted on sharing with me, we looked around and saw the restaurant was nearly empty.

I wanted to take this woman to bed in the worst way, to recapture that intimacy shared awkwardly but gleefully under the boardwalk of Long Beach, and to feel that soft, responsive body under mine.

"I'm so glad I called you," Theresa said as I paid the check.

"I'm so glad you called me," I echoed back.

Then I made my move.

"Would your parents mind if you didn't come home tonight?" I said, cocking one eyebrow and putting a shit-eating grin on my face that was the first awkward moment of the entire evening.

Theresa smiled and reached across the table to touch my arm.

"George, I'm not trying to be coy." Then she shook her head from side to side and her copper hair flamed up under the ceiling lights. "Hell, how could I be coy with the man who took my virginity? But I guess you could say that I'm still in a grieving phase, or whatever you want to call that period of adjustment when you've just ending a long-term commitment and are still licking your wounds and finding your new place in the world."

She paused and I patted her hand and gave her a reassuring smile.

"Do you mind if we take it a little slow?" she asked, still squeezing my arm.

"Not if that's the way you'd prefer it," I lied, wanting to take her right there, right then, under the table.

We drove back to her parents' house not saying much, but I marveled how even this silence seemed so natural and easy. I pulled up in front of the house and had no sooner turned the ignition off than she flew into my arms and her soft, open mouth was devouring mine. We kissed with such fierce urgency that I forgot all thoughts of waiting and wanted her right then. I was kissing her neck and fondling her breasts over her soft cashmere sweater—they were as big and round as I remembered them—when she suddenly pulled away from me and leaned against the door on her side of the car.

"This is too much like our scenes as kids," she said, laughing softly.

"Only now I've got a better car," I joked, trying to hide my frustration.

"And we're not those wild-eyed kids any more, are we?"

With any other woman I would have been furious, but Theresa was special and I reined myself in.

"I guess not," was all I could mutter.

She turned her head and looked directly at me.

"I know that sex with you would be the easiest, most exciting I've probably ever had, but, George, I'm hoping we can cut through the haze of memory and see if we really can be good friends before we jump into bed."

I was getting very nervous with the "just good friends" line, but then her eyes started to fill up with tears and I reached over to hug her.

"I really need a good friend just now," she said in a small voice like a sad little girl and I instantly wanted to protect her and care for her.

"Okay, I think I understand," I said, patting her shoulder. "Okay."

She lay with her head cradled in my arms, and we were both comfortable with another silence. Then she stirred herself.

"I should be going in," she whispered.

We spoke briefly about our upcoming schedules and agreed on meeting the following Friday.

"Do you need any help moving? I asked, recalling that she had mentioned moving to a condo in Forest Hills.

"No," she said. "I'm not taking anything from here except my clothes, but how would you like to go furniture shopping with me?"

Furniture shopping had zero appeal to me, but with her it sounded like a dazzling offer. Doing anything with her—cleaning a toilet, clipping toenails, grocery shopping—seemed like a happy prospect. I just wanted to be with her.

"Sure!" I said.

I walked her to her door and we exchanged a quick, chaste kiss and she was gone,

I went home and didn't sleep well, not because I was dreaming about Theresa Costello, but because I was consciously fantasizing about her.

XXVIII

On Friday evening Emily arrived in her new car, a blue Solaris convertible with cream leather interior—nothing but the best for her step-father's little girl, I thought derisively. Georgie and Beth seemed as excited as Emily with the new car. Their step-father had probably assured them that they, in turn, would get theirs,

"Dad, Emily drives like an old lady!" Georgie said to me immediately after our usual greeting of a hug and several pats on the back. My father, who was a good man and a dutiful parent, never showed me any affection—it just wasn't part of his manly code—and I was determined from the day Georgie was born to be open in my feelings for him. Consequently, we had kissed until he was about twelve and suddenly that started to seem awkward for him, so we retreated to the bear hug that continued to this day. Emily and Beth were hanging on either side of me, kissing my cheeks.

"Emily drives like a responsible adult who doesn't want to get in trouble with the law," I said in a mock stern voice. I was always so delighted to see my kids, to see the happy, handsome,

179

and healthy creatures they were, and to congratulate myself for producing them as my principal contribution to the world.

"Where are we going to eat?" asked Georgie, whose mind was never long away from food. "I'm starved!" At sixteen, he was already three inches taller than his old man and outweighed me by about twenty-five pounds.

"Let's have Chinese," said Beth.

"No," said Georgie. "As soon as I finish eating Chinese food, I'm hungry again. Let's have pizza."

"That's all you ever want," said Beth.

"Em, what would you like?" I asked.

"I don't care, Daddy—whatever they want is fine with me."

"Good," Georgie exclaimed, leaping in the air and pretending to be dunking a basketball, "It's pizza!"

Disappointment was clearly registered on Beth's face but she said nothing, submitting meekly to her older brother's natural tyranny.

"How about a nice steak?" I suggested, and I could see from Georgie's expression that he was open to this idea.

"Okay," he said quickly, "but I have to have mushrooms and French fries."

"No problem," I said. Emily and Beth both smiled in agreement.

We drove to the local steak house in Emily's car. She was a good driver for a kid, I thought with relief. At the restaurant the conversation flowed easily as the kids talked about school and their friends and Georgie discussed sports with me. After dinner we drove to the local Cineplex and there was a brief debate about which movie they wanted to see until I voted with the girls against Georgie's preference for some horror flick,

We settled on a comedy about high school kids. Some scenes were so raunchy that they made me feel embarrassed to be sitting with my kids watching this crap, but they didn't seem to mind at all and just took it in stride. After the movie we stopped next door at the ice cream store. Georgie, whose appetite had returned by this time, had a banana split, while Emily and Beth had a cone—one scoop—and I had a double scoop, ignoring my paunch. Back to the house where we watched *The Tonight Show* with Jay Leno, laughing at his monologue, and then it was off to bed for everyone.

Teenagers love to sleep late whenever they get the chance, and my kids were no exceptions. I finally roused them around eleven and made them breakfast, with a lot of help from both girls. Then we headed off to the high school grounds where Georgie was playing on the junior varsity football team and Beth was a cheerleader. The day turned cloudy and cold, and Emily and I sat huddled in the stands wrapped in a blanket I had brought, but we erupted with waving arms and shouts when Georgie's team made three touchdowns. Beth was clearly excited about being a cheerleader, and her natural exuberance was displayed to good advantage. Our team won the game, and then, at Georgie's insistence, we went for pizza.

For the evening's entertainment, I had rented two classic movies that I thought the kids might enjoy: *The Maltese Falcon* and *Laura*. Both pictures had detectives as heroes. Emily definitely enjoyed them, while Beth was politely noncommittal and Georgie fell asleep.

In a private moment before going to bed, Emily whispered to me that Georgie was back with Connie, his old girlfriend, and was happy again.

The kids departed early on Sunday afternoon. The house always seemed eerily quiet after their noisy departure and I missed them. Now I had a few hours left to think about my big meeting with Campion and Mason, Nadira and Senator Braxton before heading into Manhattan. These last few days, spent first with Theresa and then with my three great kids, had been a pleasant interlude, but always hovering in the back of my mind was the big showdown that was coming. Now it was drawing near and I had to admit that I was getting anxious.

XXIX

I purposely parked my car about ten blocks away from David Braxton's loft because I wanted to walk for a while and get my head ready for the evening's main event. Also on purpose I arrived twenty minutes late for the meeting as I hoped to give the Senator time to tell Campion and Mason that I was coming. I had asked him to get them there on some pretext but not to mention me until they had arrived. Maybe he could throw them off balance by expressing once again his doubts about his son's suicide.

Outside of Braxton's loft building, I saw the Senator's Lincoln town car and his driver standing a few feet away, smoking a cigarette. I hadn't smoked on my date with Theresa or when my kids were visiting and today I had not had a cigarette either, but the temptation was too great. I bummed a cigarette from the driver and enjoyed a fast smoke, hoping to calm my nerves. After all, I was about to play cat and mouse with two brilliant minds and I had never considered myself the brightest bulb on the Christmas tree— just your ordinary guy—so the contest was hardly on an even playing field. I had every right to be nervous, I told myself, which, of course, also excused my urgent need for a cigarette.

I walked into the cavernous loft apartment, led by the Senator who had buzzed me in and met me at the door when I stepped off the elevator. Campion was seated on the sprawling sofa. The beautiful Nadira was seated on a chair opposite him, on the other side of the large coffee table, where, I recalled, I had been sitting on my last visit. Mason was standing by a window.

Campion threw me an edgy smile and Mason jut nodded in my direction with that same supercilious stare he had given me on my departure from his home. It was easy to see that both men were uncomfortable.

"If there are going to be any more wild accusations by this man, Senator, I'm going to leave!" Campion said, evidently deciding to be aggressive and pointing in my direction.

The Senator sat down next to Campion and said in a stern voice, "Peter, I want to hear what Lieutenant Russo has to say."

Neither Campion nor Mason made any reply.

Nadira threw me a small smile of encouragement. She looked tired and anxious, but even in this state I could hardly take my eyes away from her beautiful face. I was sorry to put her through this emotional scene but I thought it would be better that she knew what actually happened with David, no matter how wrenching, than to spend the rest of her life with only unanswered questions and nagging doubts.

"Thank you, Senator," I said and smiled at all four people before taking out my notebook and continuing. "I just have one or two questions so that I can tie up some loose ends."

I tried to sound very casual, as though I had come to accept their version of things. I watched Campion's body sink further into the sofa in a more relaxed position. Then I changed my tone and said, "Mr. Campion, why did you lie about Senator Braxton's plane being delayed at the airport?"

Campion flinched.

"What are you talking about?" he asked dismissively.

"I'm talking about what you told me when I asked you what had happened to the notes you had written about a possible documentary—the notes on the writing paper you took from the desk at the lodge when you moved the gun. You said that when you and Senator Braxton and Mr. Mason got to the local airport for your return flight to New York with David's body, you were delayed....let me quote you here," I said, flipping several pages of my notebook until I found what I was looking for, 'a good half hour while the plane was being refueled,' and it was during that time that you read your notes and then threw them away."

All eyes were on Campion's handsome face, now noticeably flushed.

"Okay, maybe it wasn't a half hour," Campion said, clearly annoyed and waving his hand as if he was dismissing the time discrepancy as of no consequence.

I paused and looked at Senator Braxton.

"We weren't delayed at all, Peter," Senator Braxton said, staring hard at the man sitting next to him.

Campion looked at the Senator and then up at me. What happened next was unexpected. He broke out in a smile and waved his arm again.

"Alright, that was a silly fib. You caught me off guard and I didn't want to tell you anything about the note I had been writing, so I made up the story about the documentary and when you followed up with your question about where the notes were, I lied. So what!. It's my business and..."

I interrupted him,

"Then why were you looking for paper in the desk drawer where the gun was?"

Campion glanced at Mason, still standing by the window, and then said in a lower voice.

"I wanted to write a note to a lady friend and I didn't want to use my own stationery."

"And did you write this note to your lady friend?" I asked

Campion didn't answer immediately, and Senator Braxton spoke.

"Peter, with apologies to my daughter-in-law, we're men of the world. We understand these things."

Campion gave the Senator an icy smile and turned his gaze back to me.

"Yes," he said

"And did you send this note to your lady friend?" I asked.

Anger flashed in Campion's eyes

"No, I didn't. I tore it up when I got back to New York."

He threw me another icy smile, full of condescension.

I glanced at Nadira who was staring intently at Campion, but she said nothing.

This was all so neat, I thought, and decided to change the subject to keep them edgy.

"Now you said that when you heard the single shot, you were in your room writing at your desk. Is that correct?"

Campion looked like a man who was growing bored with these silly questions. He responded with a simple "Yes," and flicked some imaginary lint off his pants.

"So you were writing at the desk in your bedroom, only it wasn't some ideas for a documentary, it was a note to a lady friend. Correct?"

Sarcasm was purposely slipping into my tone as I intentionally repeated the revelation about writing a note to a lady friend. I hit the mark. Campion's demeanor changed completely. His eyes were now ablaze and his jaw muscles were twitching..

"Yes," Campion said through clenched teeth.

"Then here's my dilemma, Mr. Campion," I said, meeting his blazing stare with a calm voice and a mocking smile. "I've examined your bedroom at the lodge and your desk is right next to the interior window that looks directly down on the living room, with a full view of the spot where David Braxton died."

I paused to let everyone focus on what I was saying.

"And when you heard the shot, all you had to do was get up from your desk and take two short steps to the window and look down to see what had happened."

I paused again. Campion looked like he was going to explode.

"But you and Mr. Mason—who had a similar view of the living room from his adjacent room—both said that you rushed out of your rooms, down the stairs and through the hallway to the living room to discover David's slumped body."

Jack Mason now left the window where he had been standing all this time and moved to Campion's side but didn't sit down. His condescending smile was a mirror of the one Campion had given me before turning angry.

"Really, Lieutenant, that's an absurdly inconsequential detail. We weren't thinking, given the shocking sound of a gun going off. We were just acting on impulse."

Before I could say anything, Senator Braxton rose from where he had been sitting beside Campion and faced the two men, his eyes narrowing.

"No, Jack, that makes no sense. It seems clear to me that the natural, impulsive thing to do would be for both of you to look out your window first. Why didn't you do that?"

Mason gave the Senator a small nod.

"You're right, Senator, and I did look out my window and I saw David slumped over so I ran downstairs to get to him and…"

I interrupted him.

"That's not what you told me, Mr. Mason. Do you want me to quote you from my notes?"

"The hell with your notes!" Mason thundered.

"Why are you being so defensive?" the Senator shouted with a look of both surprise and mounting anger.

As I had hoped but could never have predicted with any assurance, Senator Braxton was becoming my ally in this confrontation, playing two against two. Nadira, her body bent forward, was listening intently to our exchanges but said nothing.

"We're not being defensive, "Campion said but his tone betrayed him. Pointing to me, he continued. "He's twisting all these nitpicking details and trying to make something monstrous out of them."

Mason now broke in.

"With all due respect, Senator, I deeply resent this inquisition and I've just about had all that I can stand."

Campion now rose from his seat, shaking his head in agreement with his friend. I sensed that a clever strategy was playing out before my eyes. I saw my quarry slipping away and decided to take a desperate leap. But before I could speak, the Senator came to my rescue, speaking in his public, authoritative voice.

"I don't find them nitpicking. I find them troubling. And out of respect for David I ask you to hear the lieutenant out." Then his voice faltered and his eyes grew moist. "I know you loved my son, just as he loved you, and I don't know what you're hiding, but

I honestly feel that you're hiding something and I beg you , I implore you, to tell me what it is."

Suddenly, this big, powerful man seemed old and helpless as he slumped down into the sofa and wiped away the tears staining his cheeks. Nadira rose from her chair and moved to sit beside him on the long, curving sofa, placing her arm around his shoulder. Mason and Campion seemed genuinely touched and, seeing my chance, I followed up in a calm voice.

"Gentlemen, I've been investigating deaths for many years now and it's just those little things—those nitpicking little things, as you call them—that start to form a pattern and then a bigger picture. For example, you both testified that you finished your drinks at the cocktail hour but all three glasses were still half- filled when I examined them three days later."

I stopped, letting this latest discrepancy in their testimony register on all three men before continuing. Mason and Campion were still standing, but both were looking distracted and uncomfortable.

I was about to take my giant leap. I took a deep breath.

"Senator, you asked me to investigate how your son died because you were convinced it wasn't suicide. Once I saw the circumstantial evidence I agreed with you. How, then, did David come to die?"

All three men and Nadira were motionless, staring at me intently. Now I sprung my trap.

"I can't provide a motive yet and I'm sketchy on some of the details but I believe that David was killed by one of his two best friends."

Both Mason and Campion sprung to life as if a bolt of lightning had passed through their bodies. Their eyes widened; their hands flew up, and they lurched toward me.

"What the hell are you saying?" Campion shouted.

"You son of a bitch!" was all Mason came up with, to express his indignation.

I remained calm and met their blazing stares.

"Mr. Mason, you told me that you were awakened from your nap by a loud bang and when you went downstairs, you found Mr. Campion already in the living room next to David's body. Since you knew that he, too, had left the living room to write in his room, you assumed that it had taken a few seconds for you to wake and get your bearings before rushing downstairs, and that was why Mr. Campion had arrived in the living room moments before you."

Now I shifted my gaze exclusively to Campion.

"Your thumbprint, Mr. Campion, was found on the gun, next to David Braxton's prints, suggesting that your hand was placed over his and somehow you forced him to pull the trigger."

"That's ridiculous!" was all Campion could muster in a scoffing tone.

"Maybe so," I said, "but we'll let the district attorney's office decide that."

Senator Braxton now rose from the sofa and, with tears in his eyes, faced Campion.

"Peter, is this true?" he asked, his voice cracking.

"Of course not, Senator," Campion said quickly. "I loved David. He was like a brother to me."

"Ever since Cain and Abel, brothers have been known to harbor secret jealousies and hatred," I said matter-of-factly.

"I told you how my thumbprint got on the gun!" Campion shouted at me, his eyes full of fury.

"Oh, yes," I said. "The paper for taking notes on an idea for a documentary that now you say was actually for writing to a lady friend but you threw it away rather than sending it." I was using my most skeptical tone. "Perhaps a grand jury will believe that story, but I don't. Especially when another *nitpicking*, as you call it, discrepancy comes into play regarding the issue of the gun handle where your print was found and the way you described how you moved the gun in the desk drawer to get at the writing paper. I'll leave that for experts to show the discrepancy there."

"Peter," Senator Braxton said, "you've been like a son to me. I don't know what to believe."

Once again, the Senator's body crumpled into the sofa. Campion sat down next to him and put his hand on the Senator's shoulder. Nadira had risen from the sofa and had walked to a window where she stood motionless, with her back to us.

"I swear to you on the life of my children that I did not kill your son," he said and now I saw tears in his eyes, too. "How could you possibly think so?"

Campion's soft tone and tearfulness were surprises to me after all his bluster and aggressive defensiveness.

Jack Mason moved to the rear of the sofa and placed his hands on both men's shoulders.

"This has gone far enough," he said, his voice loud and firm.

Campion lowered his head, as if struggling with himself.

"No, Jack! We promised David," Campion said softly.

"David is gone and these people are suffering," Mason calmly replied. "Besides, it's nothing to be ashamed of. Remember what we believe and how we practiced what we believe."

His head still bowed, Campion said, "I suppose you're right."

"Of course I'm right," Mason said. "If you're being accused of David's murder, that is something David would never have wanted. It's time to tell the truth."

Nadira now took a few steps forward from where she had been silently standing and in a pleading voice said, "Yes, please tell the truth. Please tell us what really happened."

Mason gave his friend a reassuring pat on the back and then came around the sofa and took a seat on the other side of Senator Braxton. He began speaking in a low, tired voice. Nadira returned to her place by the window but turned to face the men on the sofa. Her face was immobile, like a beautiful mask, and I saw fear in her eyes. Her arms were folded tightly across her chest. For the first time since my arrival at the loft, I sat down in the chair opposite the sofa and listened intently to an unfolding story that would haunt me for the rest of my life.

XXX

"From the time the three of us met, Peter and I felt a kinship with David and we saw that he was different. It wasn't just that he was brilliant and we could discuss any subject with him. He was also fun-loving and a superb athlete and a natural leader, loaded with charm. But he had a very serious side to him, too. He always seemed to recognize, even at thirteen, when we came together, that he had been blessed with such extraordinary good fortune—and who could deny that he had looks, brains, personality, health, a loving family, high social position, a vast inheritance and every opportunity a guy could wish for—and he had this strong desire to live life to the fullest. He infected us with his quest for the consciously lived life, especially after we all read Thoreau.

"David was heavily influenced by Buddhism and the state of enlightenment. As young as we were, and we really didn't know what we were doing, we were searching for enlightenment.

"The seeing eye of Buddha," I interjected, remembering the secret code the three boys had invented, and Mason nodded, yes.

"David wanted to do everything, to experience everything, to help the world, to be a leader, and, most of all, to achieve a full consciousness of living in the moment. Sometimes he called it mindfulness; other times, wakefulness.

"There were lots of very bright kids at Groton but they weren't into the serious stuff the way the three of us were. Then, when we got to Yale and the first course we signed up for was a philosophy course with Professor Jenkins and David really took off and we trailed right along.

"He had a hard time convincing you, Senator, that he wanted to major in philosophy, as Peter had with his father. My father put his foot down and allowed me only to minor in it, but it didn't matter. We thought of philosophy as providing paradigms for living and we were intrigued by those thinkers who sought ways of living more consciously. It was David who discovered Max Luhrs and his preoccupation with death as a stimulus for more conscious living, That's when things took a turn for the worse, I guess, but we thought at the time that we were destined to live life on a higher level, as superior intellects."

Mason halted here, as though collecting his thoughts for the next revelation, but Campion took over.

"David was convinced that the only way we could ever achieve any degree of daily wakefulness was if we were facing the real possibility of death. This seemed logical to Jack and me and as soon as we left Yale, we volunteered for Vietnam. David and I became helicopter pilots and Jack became an artillery officer. We all saw a lot of action and were mindful that we were living with death every day."

"I can relate to that," I interjected.. "I thought a lot about death when I was in Nam too. Everybody did."

Campion nodded in my direction and continued.

"David and I were sent out on rescue missions, to get men who were pinned down under enemy fire or to rescue other pilots whose choppers had been shot down. As you know, Senator, David's chopper was shot down twice. The second time, he was shot in the shoulder. We all earned a lot of medals and when we finally came home, we knew first-hand all about death. We were determined to keep that sharp image alive, not to morbidly dwell on it but, as David said, to help live our lives more fully. The three of us were out at your lodge, Senator, getting a little R & R after being discharged, before plunging back into civilian life. It was there that David came up with a plan.

"One night after Mrs Jenkowski had gone home and we were sitting around having some cognac, David said, 'Suppose you knew that you only had one year to live. How would that affect how you lived your life and what you did?'

"Of course we answered that we would want to cram as much living into our daily lives as possible, achieve as many of our goals and dreams as possible, extract the fullest degree of pleasure and satisfaction from every little event, and leave a vivid legacy for our loved ones.

"David took a sip of his drink, put the glass down and smiled.

'What if we forced ourselves to face the actual possibility of death once a year?' David said, producing a 38 revolver from his pocket and holding it in his hand.

'How?' we asked in unison, in denial of what he might be suggesting.

'The old game of Russian roulette,' he said, pointing the gun at the side of his head. 'Think about it: one chance out of six that the one bullet would be in the chamber that you discharge. Five out of six chances that it wouldn't be. Those aren't bad odds, but still, if we knew at the end of each one-year period that there was the real possibility of dying, wouldn't that be the greatest spur to extracting as much from each day, each minute in that year as you possibly could?'"

Campion paused and Mason took over again.

"Naturally, we were shocked at this proposal but as we talked about it and thought about it more during our time together at the lodge, it made perfect sense, for our goals in life were beyond those of most men. Living in the shadow of an untimely death would certainly stimulate us to both wakefulness and accelerated achievements. It probably sounds insane to you, Senator, and you, Lieutenant, and surely you, Nadira, but we wanted to live life on a higher plane and we saw this plan as helping us to achieve our goal.

"Our last night at the lodge, David again produced the gun.

'I've marked one of the six chambers with a dot, to indicate where the one bullet would be. Let's spin the cylinder and see what would happen if we pretend the bullet is in that marked chamber.'

"He spun the cylinder and immediately placed the gun next to his temple and pulled the trigger. Then he opened the cylinder and smiled.

'I'd be good for another year,' he said.

"He spun the cylinder again and passed it to Peter. After a little hesitation, Peter, too, placed the gun to his temple and pulled the trigger, and then returned the gun to David for examination.

'Another year for you, too, Peter,' David said cheerfully.

"Now I imitated the actions of my two friends and David pronounced another year for me, too.

'But, of course,' Peter said, placing the revolver back on the coffee table, 'this is meaningless without the one bullet. Suppose we plan on returning here next year—just the three of us—for some hunting and fishing, and then we'll play the real version of Russian roulette.'

"We all agreed and the die was cast.

"Immediately upon my return home, I found myself thinking about what I could be facing in 364 short days and, as David had predicted, life took on much more meaning. I was easily able to focus on the immediate present, to see everything in richer tones and broader perspectives, to appreciate my family and friends more and to not waste a day, an hour, a minute without advancing some goal or responding to some spontaneous thought. I never felt more alive or more fulfilled. When I spoke to David or Peter, it was the same for them. We were joyfully racing through life yet conscious of every second.

"The year passed quickly and we returned to the lodge with the understanding that the men we had become in this past year— our achievements and fulfillment, our enlarged natures and eagerness for experiences, our enhanced empathy and capacity for caring, had all been predicated on what we had agreed to face at this point.

"On the last night of our stay, we fortified ourselves with a few drinks and David produced the revolver. We watched in silence as he also produced a bullet and placed it in a chamber and spun the cylinder rigorously. With little hesitation he placed the gun at his temple and pulled the trigger. The click I heard seemed to reverberate endlessly around the room.

"David laughed. 'Another year!' he said.

"We had faced death many times in Vietnam but this was different because it was self-selected rather than random; yet, we knew that this plan of action had immeasurably enriched our lives and I guess we were full of hubris, thinking ourselves more enlightened and superior to other people—those millions of men who live lives of quiet desperation, as Thoreau observed.

"First I, then Peter, spun the cylinder, squeezed the trigger and registered immense relief when a click was the only response. And each year since then, we've followed our plan and played our annual game until finally the one-in-six chance wasn't on our side and David's luck ran out."

Mason's voice trailed off and we all sat in silence, each with his own thoughts.

"How utterly stupid! Stupid and senseless!" Senator Braxton exclaimed, rising from the sofa and walking to a window, where he turned and faced us. "What a horrible waste! I just don't understand how anyone with any brains could do such a thing! Such a stupid waste!"

He suddenly looked very old as his face became a mask of misery. He turned away from us, embarrassed.

"I know it's hard for anyone to understand," Campion said. "That's why we wouldn't say anything to anyone. Truthfully, if it got out to the press, my career would be ruined. We were so shocked and confused that we quickly decided to pass it off as an inexplicable suicide rather than reveal the circumstances of an accidental suicide. But you got Lieutenant Russo on the case and he saw the discrepancies in our story. I'm so sorry, Senator."

"Even when a brilliant mind makes up lies, an average but trained mind can spot them," I said, recognizing an unexpected pomposity in my voice. I continued. "So that explains why the whiskey glasses were only half empty and why the whole story about going upstairs was made up."

Mason nodded. The Senator turned toward me.

"What about Peter's thumbprint on the gun?" he asked.

Before I had a chance to answer, Campion spoke.

"Every year we followed a ritual of reversing the order in which the three of us played the game. This year I was first and David was next. His finger prints must have covered all of mine except for the thumbprint."

"The forensic report said that while David's prints were clearly discernible, there were other smudged prints below his," I added.

Senator Braxton now spoke in a louder voice, having regained some of the magisterial power he wielded in his public life. Ignoring me, he spoke directly to Mason and Campion.

"I know that my son was the leader of your little pack so I can't blame you for influencing him, but all three of you were brilliant minds and not one of you had the sense to see how senseless this was?"

"We saw it from a different perspective," was all Campion could say.

"And you never planned on the possibility of this happening, and the aftermath for the rest of us who loved you?" the Senator asked, his voice cracking.

"We had all written letters to our wives that we entrusted to our lawyers if the time ever came when we lost the game," Mason said. "Without stating specifically what we were doing, we wanted them to know how much we loved them and how fulfilled we felt in our lives."

Nadira now moved forward from the window and stood directly in front of Campion and Mason. When she spoke, her voice was hard and her eyes were blazing with anger.

"Just what was that letter supposed to do? It didn't give me any answers to my questions or lighten my distress. If anything, it left me more confused and distraught." Her arms fell to her side and now her voice broke and she wailed, "I can't believe that you were willing to throw away your lives for some abstract philosophical idea!"

"It wasn't abstract to us," Campion said in a clearly defensive tone. "It became the code by which we dared to live."

"I think the reality was that we never thought we wouldn't beat the odds," Mason said. "and we were concentrating on summoning our coverage to face the game each year. I guess that in the back of our minds we knew this could happen, but we mostly suppressed that possibility. We had been so lucky in every other aspect of our lives, and this yearly routine had been such a spur to living more fully and appreciating everything so much more."

"And now, with David dead, do you still see this from the same perspective?" the Senator said, his voice rising in anger.

Mason exchanged glances with Campion before answering.

"No, Senator. The game is ended."

"Then at least some good can come of this, but at such an awful price," the Senator said, his voice faltering again and deep sorrow contorting his face. He turned to me.

"Thank you, Lieutenant, for your help. I hope we can rely on your discretion. My son was brilliant and saw life in a different way, but I don't think the world would understand any of this. I barely do. We'll all just have to let the suicide story stand."

The Senator turned to his daughter-in-law.

"Do you agree, Nadira?"

She looked like a woman in total shock but I saw a light flickering in her eyes and her strong jaw had a resolute set.

"I don't want my children to know this. Perhaps I'll explain it when they're grown up, although I'll have to struggle with explaining it to myself first. For now, we'll leave it as an unfathomable suicide. People simply would not understand the real motivation behind this action, and I don't want David's life to become the butt of jokes."

Her eyes glistened with tears as she stared at Campion and Mason.

"I only wish that...that one of you..." She stopped speaking and turned back to the window. I watched her shoulders quivering as she tried to muffle her sobs. I wanted more than anything to rush to her side, take her in my arms and comfort her, but I resisted this temptation. Senator Braxton went to her and she lay her head on his shoulder. The rest of us watched in silence as these two brave people, united in their overwhelming grief, struggled to console each other. No one spoke for several minutes until finally the Senator turned his eyes to Mason and Campion.

"Are we all in agreement, gentlemen?"

All three of us nodded, yes.

Gazing about the apartment as if he were envisioning his son again, he said, " Then the truth dies here."

XXXI

The Senator's Lincoln town car and driver were waiting at the curb when we all exited the building.

"Can I give you a lift, Lieutenant?" He asked..

"No thanks, Senator. I'd like to walk for a while."

He thanked me again and we shook hands, and I saw such pain in his eyes that I quickly looked away.

It had been raining while we were in the apartment and now it had stopped. The air smelled fresh and the watery sheen on the streets reflected the streetlights. I sucked in the air greedily and tried to clear my head. I felt as though I had been to the land of Oz. I had journeyed through the realm of the very rich and powerful and only gradually had I discovered the total personality and character of David Braxton. With every step in that discovery my mind had thrown his life in relief while highlighting my own. The contrast was startling.

David represented everything one could wish to be. He was brilliant, rich handsome, well connected, loving and loved. I was average and poor, especially after my divorce, and ordinary looking and had no powerful connections. In his short life span he had done or achieved a thousand more noteworthy things than I ever dreamed of doing. Life for me was plowing through every day, doing my job, caring about my kids and, after Ginny's death, struggling with loneliness. But David's brilliance led him to view life from a perspective that most people would say was a form of madness.

Was it madness? Does a genius see things that no ordinary person can understand? I wondered. David's "madness" seemed to spur him on to a sharper awareness of life and deeper pleasure in his moment-to-moment pursuits. He was living life on the edge, challenging the gods to bring him down, and they did. I thought of his beautiful widow, his dazed young children and his grieving parents and relatives. Was there just a split second, I wondered, when the bullet left the chamber and pierced his brain—one brief second before everything went blank—when he thought about them and regretted this tragic game?

Then a poem that I had memorized in high school popped into my head—a poem that my crazy junior-year English teacher, Mrs. Collins, had insisted we all learn by heart and each one of us had to stand in front of the class and recite it. I never forgot it. It was the only poem I knew by heart It was called "Richard Cory" by Edwin Arlington Robinson. Walking toward my car in the glistening city streets I recited it to myself.

> Whenever Richard Cory went down town,
>
> We people on the pavement looked at him:
>
> He was a gentleman from sole to crown,

Clean favored, and imperially slim.

And he was always quietly arrayed,

And he was always human when he talked;

But still he fluttered pulses when he said,

"Good morning," and he glittered when he walked.

And he was rich—yes, richer than a king—

And admirably schooled in every grace:

In fine, we thought that he was everything

To make us wish that we were in his place.

So on we worked, and waited for the light,

And went without the meat, and cursed the bread;

And Richard Cory, one calm summer night,

Went home and put a bullet through his head.

I supposed David Braxton was like Richard Cory who, for all his gifts and blessings, could not muddle through life like the rest of us. I couldn't say that I had many moments of conscious happiness in my current life, except maybe when I was with my kids or having a beer with some of my buddies from the detective squad, or the evening I spent with Theresa—all wonderful moments but nothing spectacular or earth shaking. But being able to sort of step outside yourself and see yourself and the people surrounding you having an enjoyable time, gave you an extra measure of pleasure in what you were doing. You felt the moment more intensely. I guessed that this was what David Braxton would call "wakefulness."

Maybe Braxton and all those philosophers he read were on to something when they preached about every waking minute being important Maybe I could try to be more aware of living in the present, like I was when I was in Nam. Then I thought of all the ordinary, everyday things I did—all the paperwork that I detested and shopping for groceries and doing the laundry and cutting my toenails and getting my car serviced—all not high on my enjoyment list. My next thought was that Braxton had the luxury of having other people do these things for him if he wished, so he had the freedom to live life on a higher plane and make most of his days consciously happy and satisfying ones. For the rest of us, "…on we worked and waited for the light."

I'd give it some more thought later but right now I craved a cigarette. I spotted an open deli half a block away and headed for it. I'd buy one last pack of cigarettes and when they were gone, I'd definitely quit. Finished! Over! The End!

I walked faster toward the deli, anticipating how much I would consciously enjoy that first drag on the cigarette. I could taste the smoke being drawn into my mouth, circling around my tongue before descending to my lungs and then billowing out my nose.

Yes, that first drag was going to be special and I'd savor it. I'd call it a David Braxton moment.

XXXII

Contrary to what Senator Braxton said on the night that we unraveled the mystery of David Braxton's death and he swore Mason, Campion, Nadira and me to secrecy, asserting that "the truth dies here," the truth did not die. It just lay unrevealed for a long time.

I have written this true story of how David Braxton died because the truth must eventually be told. I have placed it in my safety deposit box with instructions to my wife Theresa and my daughter Emily that it is not to be made public until twenty-five years after my death. Even at that advanced date I'm sure that this revelation will be painful to David's relatives but I consider that issue to be of secondary importance when compared to the lessons that David's life can teach all of us.

In the years since 1994 when I investigated David's life and philosophic outlook, I have thought of him frequently. While his intense desire to experience the gift of life to the fullest capacity was a worthy life-goal, the extreme means by which he chose to stimulate his focus on day-to-day living was self-defeating.

A far better example of living according to one's philosophy would be Professor Jenkins. I intentionally kept in contact with him until his death in 2007, and, to his great credit, he welcomed the friendship of an ordinary man like myself. We didn't talk about philosophy; we didn't have to. He was curious about all aspects of life and seemed to thoroughly enjoy hearing of my experiences as a detective. He wanted to know all about my children's progress and my newly found happiness in my marriage to Theresa. In the course of our conversations through the ensuing years, I learned that because of a very early cancerous condition Hildi was forced to have a hysterectomy and they could never have children.

"We thought about adopting," he said, giving me that megawatt smile with pinpoints of light dancing in his eyes, "but we were surrounded by an endless stream of bright young students whom we could interact with and, we hoped, influence, and then there were the special ones who really became like family."

His smile became more wistful and I knew, of course, that he was referring to the three friends. He told me that Peter Campion and Jack Mason still kept in touch with him and occasionally visited, which made him very happy, and that Senator Braxton had sold the lodge in Idaho shortly after his son's death.

He once casually confessed to me that although he had done very well academically in earning his graduate degrees at Ivy League universities and had risen to the rank of full professor at

Yale, he had never considered himself among the highest rank of brilliant theoreticians or creative minds.

"My success aligns with Edison's observation that 'Genius is one per cent inspiration and ninety-nine per cent perspiration.' Nothing came easily to me; I had to work hard for everything I achieved. That's why I had great appreciation, even awe, for unique minds like David's. They're very rare, almost a freak of nature, like Thomas Carlyle or Einstein or Stephen Hawking, and I'm fascinated with them and the ends to which they apply their brilliance."

To me, it was a humbling experience for this exceptional man to have such a genuinely modest self-appraisal, especially when I thought of my own life and accomplishments. I was also flattered that he thought enough of me to share such confidences. Like an innocent child, he had freed his mind of any prejudices or pre-conceived notions about anyone he encountered. He possessed a rare gift for friendship with all sorts of people whom he eagerly explored for their individual, life-enhancing qualities, no matter how meager or hidden, as in my case. I was drawn to him like a magnet.

His great zest for living was apparent in everything he did. He was a living example of joyful "wakefulness," without the need to create a harrowing dark side as a spur to living life fully. He, rather than David Braxton, should be a model we could all imitate in enriching our lives.

Of course, Professor Jenkins knew what had really happened that night at the lodge in Idaho, but we never spoke of it directly. He mourned David as he would mourn a son—a brilliant son who had been carried away with an excess of pride and intensity. I remember one time when he was talking about some singular exploit of David's and he quoted a few lines of poetry that he felt summarized David's life. They stuck with me.

> My candle burns at both ends,
>
> It will not last the night,
>
> But, oh, my friends and, oh, my foes,
>
> It casts a lovely light.

Then I thought back to that one line from Thoreau that Professor Jenkins had written in the margin of Braxton's senior term paper: "It is characteristic of wisdom not to do desperate things."

David Braxton had brilliance; Professor Jenkins had wisdom. Perhaps you don't have to be very smart to be wise. As we muddle through life, there's hope for us all.

George Russo
2008

CPSIA information can be obtained at www.ICGtesting.com
Printed in the USA
266726BV00001B/50/P